Message in a Bottle

A Julie Mystery

by Kathryn Reiss

American Girl®

Published by American Girl Publishing

17 18 19 20 21 22 23 24 25 LEO 10 9 8 7 6 5 4 3 2 1

Cover image by Juliana Kolesova and Joe Hinrichs

Cataloging-in-Publication Data available from the Library of Congress.

For the real Raymond and real Dolores,
our son and daughter who like to see
their names in print,
with love

And to my patient editor extraordinaire,
Judith Woodburn,
thank you!

BeForever™

The adventurous characters you'll meet in
the BeForever books will spark your curiosity
about the past, inspire you to find your voice
in the present, and excite you about your future.
You'll make friends with these girls as you share
their fun and their challenges. Like you, they are
bright and brave, imaginative and energetic,
creative and kind. Just as you are, they are
discovering what really matters: Helping others.
Being a true friend. Protecting the earth.
Standing up for what's right. Read their stories,
explore their worlds, join their adventures.
Your friendship with them will BeForever.

TABLE *of* CONTENTS

chapter 1
Desperately Needed

"I STILL CAN'T believe it!" Mrs. Albright said as she and Julie crept through heavy traffic on their way out of San Francisco. They edged toward the Bay Bridge, which would take them across the bay, then north to the mountains.

"I know." Julie snapped her fingers. "Long-lost relatives out of thin air!"

"Not really long lost," Julie's mom said. "But it *has* been a very long time . . ." Her voice trailed off as a taxi blared its horn, and an ambulance screamed past. She rubbed her forehead. "Sitting here in traffic, I think my sister had the right idea about getting away from all this!"

Julie reached for the envelope sticking out of her mom's purse on the seat between them.

She unfolded the single sheet of notepaper and squinted at her aunt's loopy script.

Hey there, big sis,

I know it's been forever, but I'm writing to invite you to visit us at Gold Moon Ranch. Your girls can hang out with my Raymond!

We don't have a phone here at the ranch, but I'm enclosing driving directions so you can find us. Can you come right away? Like . . . NOW*? The truth is, I desperately need your help.*

Love,

Nadine

Julie tried to picture her aunt Nadine and cousin Raymond in her head but came up blank. She hadn't seen them since she was a toddler, and all she knew was what her mother had shared from Aunt Nadine's infrequent letters. Aunt Nadine had dropped out of college to get married and start a commune with her husband. The commune was a group of people who wanted to live far from the modern world with all its troubles—its wars, pollution, and hectic pace. They wanted to live close to nature and grow their own food. They had set up their own community, called Gold Moon Ranch, in the Sierra mountains. Its nearest neighbor was a tiny town called Sonora, which had once been a lively gold-mining town and was now a popular tourist spot. Since moving to the commune, Aunt Nadine had rarely returned to San Francisco.

"Now, after all this time, she 'desperately' wants to see you," Julie mused. "I wonder why?" She felt a thrill as their car inched along onto the bridge that led out of the crowded city.

Aunt Nadine's invitation was the most interesting thing to have happened all summer. Julie's friends Ivy and CJ were out of town visiting relatives. Her older sister, Tracy, worked two summer jobs and was hardly ever home. Summer vacation was nearly over now, and Julie had spent most of it on the living room couch working her way through stacks of library books. She was excited at the thought of getting to know her cousin Raymond, who seemed to live such a different life from hers. She tucked her feet under her on the seat and gazed out the window at all the traffic on the bridge. *I wonder if he and I will be friends?* She hoped so.

Julie knew her mother was eager to see her sister again, too. When the letter from Aunt Nadine arrived, Mrs. Albright quickly arranged for her assistant to fill in at Gladrags, the shop where she sold beaded jewelry, mobiles, lava lamps, and used clothing that she'd refashioned into trendy styles. Mrs. Albright also arranged for Tracy to stay with Dad. He was an airline pilot who lived on the other side of the city, and the girls visited him whenever his flight schedule allowed. Julie and her mom packed their suitcases and set off just two days after receiving Aunt Nadine's note.

The car picked up speed along the highway to the hills, and as the smell of the summer air blowing in her window changed from the exhaust of cars and trucks to a fishy saltwater tang off the San Francisco Bay, Julie found it hard to stay awake. She dozed in the car until her rumbling stomach woke her. Their station wagon was winding up a narrow mountain road.

"Good timing," Mrs. Albright said, glancing over at Julie. "We're just passing through Sonora. Not too much farther to the ranch." Her hands gripped the steering wheel tightly.

"Don't worry, Mom," Julie said. "Aunt Nadine will be happy to see us!"

"It feels strange to arrive without phoning first."

Julie looked out the window at the brick and stone buildings lining Sonora's main street. The historic homes with iron shutters and ornate fences nestled in old-fashioned gardens made Julie feel as though they were driving through a movie set about the old West. "Back when these houses were built, I bet people didn't have phones," she said. "They couldn't call ahead either."

"Good point," Mrs. Albright said. "I'm sure it will be fine. But we've surely missed lunchtime there . . . so how about stopping for a snack?"

"Yum!" Julie was ready for a break.

At the end of the main street, a flashing rocket-shaped sign announced the Galaxy Cafe. The claim on the board below it sounded promising: *Our Meals Are Out of This World!* They parked and walked into the low, modern building.

Julie's eyes widened at the gleaming chrome-and-glass tables and shiny chairs. The dark blue ceiling twinkled with stars, and a mobile of the Skylab space station dangled from it, rotating slowly. "Cool!" she exclaimed. They took a table near the door and waited. And waited.

"Don't they have waiters in the future?" Julie joked after a few minutes.

Finally, a teenage waitress with warm brown skin and a cloud of dark hair arrived at their table with an apologetic smile. "Sorry to keep you waiting!" The air around her held a delicate scent of flowers.

Julie smiled back. The girl's name tag proclaimed: Hi, I'm DOLORES. She wore black pants, a black T-shirt, and a metallic silver apron. She laid silverware and paper napkins printed with little red rockets at each of their places, then drew an order pad from the apron pocket, which also sported an embroidered red rocket. "What'll it be?"

"I'll have the Apollo Cheeseburger and Gemini Fries, please," Julie said.

Mrs. Albright was giving her order for Cosmic Vegetable Soup when a red-faced balding man wearing round wire-rimmed glasses strode from the kitchen to their table. "Dolores, this won't do." He consulted a rocket-shaped watch. "Your break is twenty minutes, not thirty."

"I'm sorry, Mr. Coker," the waitress said, her smile strained. "It won't happen again."

"Don't just *say* sorry, *show* sorry," Mr. Coker snapped.

Cheeks flaming, Dolores hurried to the kitchen. Julie was embarrassed for the girl. It was bad enough to get in trouble with your boss, but even worse to be scolded in front of customers! She wouldn't want him for a boss.

A short time later, Dolores was back with a tray of food. Mr. Coker approached their table with a critical eye.

"One vegetable soup," Dolores said, setting a bowl in front of Mrs. Albright. "And one grilled cheese," she said to Julie.

Julie and her mother looked at each other. "Um, it was supposed to be—" Julie began. She bit her lip, but not soon enough to keep Mr. Coker from plucking the order pad from Dolores's apron pocket and scanning the page impatiently.

"Cheeseburger and fries is what the young lady ordered."

"It's okay . . ." Julie blurted out. "I like grilled cheese, too."

Dolores snatched up the plate and bolted for the kitchen.

"It *is* a problem, I'm afraid," Mr. Coker said, shaking his head. "It's not the impression I want to leave you with, as the owner of this restaurant. Sonora may be full of Gold Rush history, but I look to the future. I'm trying to build a business. That not only means good food, it means good service!"

His voice was calm, but he watched with narrowed eyes as the door to the kitchen swung shut behind Dolores. "There will be no charge for this meal. I'm sorry for the confusion."

He changed the subject before Mrs. Albright could protest. "Traveling far today?"

"We're from San Francisco," Julie told him. "We're going to Gold Moon Ranch."

Mr. Coker raised his eyebrows. "Joining the hippies?"

"Just visiting," replied Mrs. Albright.

"It's not the place it used to be," said Mr. Coker. "There used to be a large community, and they were quite self-sufficient. But now they're having to get jobs like the rest of us." He tipped his head toward the table where Dolores was now delivering the grilled cheese to the person who had ordered it. "Your waitress lives there. She doesn't have much practical experience, but I'm trying to give her a chance. She wants to help their community, and goodness knows, they need the money!" He shook his head. "High time they rejoined civilization. I've made a very good offer to buy their land, but so far they aren't interested in selling. I'll keep trying. They'll see reason soon enough!"

He turned abruptly. "Now, let me see what's holding up your order."

A few moments later, Dolores returned with

Julie's cheeseburger and fries. She set the food on the table and gave Julie a smile. "I couldn't help hearing what you said. It will be nice to have another girl at the ranch for a while." Then she leaned in and lowered her voice. "I also heard what Mr. Coker said! He has as much chance of buying Gold Moon Ranch as I have of . . . of keeping this stupid job. We'll never sell, no matter how desperate we get!"

She turned on her heel and disappeared back through the swinging doors. Julie picked up a French fry from her plate and blew on it thoughtfully. Dolores was the second person from the commune to mention being desperate. What on earth was happening at Gold Moon Ranch?

chapter 2

Bad Luck

BACK IN THE car, Mrs. Albright peered at the driving directions. "Turn off one mile beyond the cafe. Look for a red wooden gate on the left."

Julie watched the sides of the road, wondering about the aunt and cousin who would be waiting for them. Why did Aunt Nadine need Julie's mom so desperately?

"There!" Julie pointed out a sagging red gate, half hidden by bushes.

Mrs. Albright turned the car sharply up a steep, unpaved drive. At the top of the drive, she parked in a circle of gravel next to two old cars and a battered van. Just beyond the parking area, a large, ramshackle house stood in the shelter of pine trees. It had a long front porch, a tin roof, and two tall stone chimneys. The weathered boards of the house were unpainted, but Julie liked the bright blue front door and the cascades of herbs from the window boxes. The smell of rosemary and mint grew stronger as they walked up to the house. Julie tapped on the door, but no one came.

Mrs. Albright knocked harder. "We come all this way, and they're not even home?" she muttered.

Julie peered through one of the windows into a large room. Four long tables were set for dinner. Loaves of bread and plates of sliced tomatoes lay on one. But the mismatched chairs surrounding the tables were empty. No one was there.

"Looks like they left in the middle of cooking," Julie said.

"Odd," said Mrs. Albright.

Julie jumped off the porch and looked around. After a moment, the silence was broken by shouts coming from some distance away, followed by a screech, and then: "Don't let her escape!"

Intrigued, Julie followed the voices across a small meadow, passing a garden full of tomato plants and squash growing tall over high trellises. She reached two barns both surrounded by a low rail fence. At the edge of the barnyard, people raced this way and that, stooping down, then standing up with something in their arms that seemed to be flapping and clucking.

"Look, Mom. Chickens!"

Mrs. Albright stopped and put her hands to her face. "Oh! There's Nadine!" She started laughing. "She looks just the same!"

A tall, thin woman with long, fair hair the color of Julie's stepped away from the group, thrusting the chicken she held into the arms of a boy about Julie's age. Then she waved and ran toward Julie and her mother, her multicolored skirt swirling around her legs.

"Joyce?" She caught Julie's mom in a bear hug

and spun her around. "Joyce, it's *you*!" Nadine's voice was husky. "Let me look at you!"

"Can it really be nearly ten years?" murmured Julie's mom, her hands tightly clasping Nadine's. "Oh, Nadine, it's good to see you! Julie, meet your Aunt Nadine."

"Hello, honeypot." The woman's smile looked so much like her mom's that Julie couldn't help but grin back. "I wanted to welcome you both properly, but as you can see we're in a bit of a pickle here." She motioned to the boy who held the chicken in his arms. "Raymond! Come meet your aunt and cousin."

The boy moved closer. He appeared to be about ten or eleven, with dark eyes and a shock of dark hair. He wore faded jeans and a blue T-shirt that hung on his thin frame. He gave Julie a fleeting smile. The chicken clucked and pecked lightly at his shoulder.

"Hi," he muttered. He moved back a step when

Julie's mother reached out to hug him.

"Hi!" Julie said cheerfully. Raymond probably didn't meet many new people, she decided.

Aunt Nadine linked her arm through her sister's. "I know you must have been surprised to get my letter, Joyce. I wasn't sure you'd come. But I know you can help us. In fact, you can start right now, with these birds! Somehow, the coop door was left open and our hens have escaped. We need to get them back in before the foxes and coyotes come out."

"If Pa were here," said Raymond in a low, tight voice, "he'd capture them in a flash."

Aunt Nadine frowned at him. "Your pa's not here. We'll catch them ourselves!"

Julie eyed the bird in Raymond's arms. She'd never held a chicken before, but this one looked placid enough. "I can help."

"Then follow me." Carrying the chicken, Raymond strode ahead to the wood-and-wire mesh enclosure and shooed it inside, latching the gate carefully. "Just put 'em in here when you get 'em."

People dashed this way and that, trying to intercept the hens that were scattering into the meadow. Julie approached a fat bird sitting under a bush and held out her hand. "Here, girl," she called, as if to a dog. The chicken studied her warily. Julie darted forward, arms outstretched—but the bird flapped its wings in panic and flew off, squawking. "I didn't know chickens could fly!" Julie exclaimed.

Raymond snorted. "Try this," he said. He walked to a wooden barrel of chicken feed, dipped in his hand, then scattered the feed on the ground. "My pa trained these hens when they were chicks. They'll come to you. They just need a little bit of encouragement!"

When two hens ventured over to peck at the feed, Raymond bent down and expertly scooped one up under each arm. He held them against his sides as he walked back toward the coop. "Your turn!" he called back to Julie.

Julie took a handful of the feed from the barrel. The chicken she'd tried to catch earlier was now sitting on a wooden fence post. Julie scattered the grain at the base of the post and then waited, not moving a muscle. The chicken eyed her suspiciously. "Here, chick," Julie cooed. "Come on, girl!"

When the hen finally hopped down to peck at the grain, Julie held her breath. Bending low and moving slowly, she grabbed the bird as Raymond had done. She tried to tuck the hen snugly against her body but found herself clutching a flapping fury of feathers. "Oh no!" cried Julie. "She's escaping!"

The others chuckled, and Julie felt her face grow pink. Determined not to embarrass herself, she wrapped her arms firmly around the struggling bird. Suddenly the bird went quiet and still in her arms. *Now I've killed it!* Julie thought. She almost dropped the bird—and then felt a gentle peck on her arm and looked down to see the chicken's beady eye fixed on her. "Good girl!" said Julie, relief coursing through her. She carried the chicken to the coop, where Raymond waited, grinning now.

"You're a natural—for a city girl!" he said.

She felt the sudden warmth of his approval and smiled back.

After that, catching chickens seemed easy. Julie placed the last one in the chicken coop, latched the door, and went to join her mother and Aunt Nadine, sighing with satisfaction. *There!* The hens were safe. Still, feathers littered the barnyard as if there had been a terrible struggle, and Julie thought a feather would make a funny souvenir of her first day's adventure at Gold Moon Ranch. Spotting an especially white one, she bent down to pick it up.

It was not a feather at all. It was a bit of crumpled white paper, and when Julie unfolded it, she saw something familiar printed on one side—a rocket headed toward the sun.

"Look, Mom, it's a napkin from that cafe!"

"May I see that?" A woman with blond braids strode over and took the napkin from Julie's hand before Julie's mother could reply. The woman studied the napkin intently. "I'd say this proves it."

"Proves what?" Julie stared at the woman in confusion.

"Vicky's got a theory," Aunt Nadine explained, "that somebody's trying to make us want to sell our land."

The woman named Vicky held up the napkin so others could see it. "Draw your own conclusions. But when I see a napkin from Coker's restaurant, I can't help but think he's been sneaking around our property, causing trouble."

"We don't know for sure it's Eli Coker—other people sometimes go to his cafe," said a young woman with a baby on her hip.

"One of us might have left the gate to the chicken pen open by mistake," said a black-bearded man with hair in dreadlocks. His eyes were tired.

"Maybe we all just need to be more careful," said a tall woman in a flowing red caftan.

The group started back to the large building they called the Big House, but Aunt Nadine drew Julie and Mrs. Albright aside. "We'll come soon," Aunt Nadine told the others.

The woman in the red caftan waved them away. "Don't worry. Bonnie and I can handle dinner prep, and Dolores will be home from the cafe soon." She smiled at Julie. "I'm Rose. My daughter will be glad of another girl at the ranch."

"Oh, you're Dolores's mom?" said Julie. "We met at the cafe!"

"Yes, and that's my husband, Allen." She pointed to the man with the dark beard and dreadlocks, who was pulling Julie's suitcase out of the station wagon. "He'll bring your bags to Nadine's cottage for you."

Julie and her mother followed Aunt Nadine

and Raymond along the path to the cottages. First they stopped at the bathhouse, where Aunt Nadine showed them the toilets, which were nothing more than pits in the ground with seats over them. She demonstrated how to use a hand pump to draw water for washing. There were six long sinks, like metal troughs, and a few metal tubs. Julie stared at her face in the mirror. She washed her hands in cold water and shivered to think of taking a bath here. Then she saw there was a fireplace and large cauldron for heating the water. A warm bath seemed like a lot of work.

Cottages lined both sides of the path, each built to the same simple plan, with a front porch and two windows. Aunt Nadine and Raymond led the way to the last cottage at the edge of the woods.

Julie stepped into a small living room. There was a single bedroom beyond, and a ladder that Julie scrambled up to find a long sleeping loft with a bed on one side and a camp cot on the other. A rolled-up sleeping bag lay on top of the cot.

Julie peered down over the edge of the loft.

"You'll be up there with Raymond," Aunt Nadine called up to her. "Joyce, you'll take my room."

"The couch is fine," Mrs. Albright protested.

"Nope—dibs on the couch!"

Julie's mother laughed. "We'll flip a coin, just like in the old days!"

"Heads I win, tails you lose?"

"Oh, Nadine, I've missed you so much . . ."

"And I've missed you," her sister answered.

Raymond spun away and slammed out onto the porch. Julie scrambled down the ladder and followed him outside. "What's wrong?" she asked.

He sank down onto the porch step and stared out at the woods. "I just wish Ma missed Pa as much as she says she's missed your mom." Through his shaggy dark hair, Julie could see his anguished expression. It was suddenly clear what he'd meant earlier when he'd wished his father could help round up the chickens.

Julie sat next to him. "My parents are divorced, too," she offered. "I used to wish they'd get back together, but now . . . well, I can see they're happier as things are."

Raymond's eyes were hard with misery. "Well, my parents are *not* divorced! And they're *not* happy as they are! None of us is happy." He jumped up when Aunt Nadine opened the screen door and their moms stepped out onto the porch.

"Lemonade, anyone?" Aunt Nadine offered. "I'm sorry it's not cold, but the only time we have ice is in the winter, when we can break icicles off the eaves." She laughed, passing glasses to Julie, her mother, and Raymond. "But who wants cold lemonade in the winter?"

Raymond scowled at his mother, but he accepted the glass and drank thirstily.

Julie took a sip of her lemonade. She was thirsty

too, and even warm it tasted delicious. Still, she couldn't imagine not having ice when she wanted it, or lights, or hot showers. "Don't you miss electricity?" she asked her aunt shyly. "Or running water?"

"We use the pump to get water," Aunt Nadine said, "and we heat it in our fireplace, and bathe in those tin tubs. We light lanterns when it's dark. Living simply isn't a problem."

Mrs. Albright set down her glass and looked at her sister kindly. "Well, then, what is the problem? We're thrilled to be here, but we're *desperate* to know why you need my help!"

Aunt Nadine sat in one rocking chair and motioned to the other. "Sit down, and I'll tell you our tale of woe." She rocked back and forth for a moment. "Nothing's gone right here for a long time. It's been this way since the war."

"The war?" Julie frowned. The Vietnam War had ended three years ago. How could it still be causing problems in a commune in the mountains?

"I'm afraid so." Aunt Nadine rubbed her forehead wearily. "David—my husband who wouldn't kill a fly!—enlisted in the army." There was a catch in her voice. "He had his reasons, but he had some awfully good reasons not to go, too. He had Raymond. And me. And this community we built. There's been trouble here ever since."

Raymond set his lemonade glass onto the step so hard, Julie was surprised the jar didn't break. "I hate when you blame everything on Pa!"

"It's been difficult," Aunt Nadine murmured.

"I miss Pa!" Raymond said abruptly. He leaped off the porch and darted down the path, vanishing among the trees.

Julie looked at her aunt in alarm, but Aunt Nadine shook her head. "He'll be back," she said. "He just misses David. But he doesn't understand."

"I'm not sure I do, either," Mrs. Albright said.

"We were all against the war in Vietnam, so it shocked me when David joined up." Aunt Nadine's voice broke. "Then he was wounded and spent months in rehabilitation trying to walk again. He couldn't do his work here on the ranch, so he took a part-time job at the library in town. He lives in Sonora because things have been strained between us. I can't help feeling angry."

Julie listened, feeling troubled. Poor Raymond!

After a pause, Aunt Nadine spoke again. "Raymond visits David a couple of times a week, but it's never enough for Raymond. He just wants his pa living here at the ranch. But David needs a desk job now. And it's hard to work out the problems between us when there are so many other problems to solve here."

"What kind of problems?" Mrs. Albright asked.

"Well, the biggest problem at the ranch is money. With David away in Vietnam, a lot of our members started leaving, too. Now our numbers are really down. It's been harder to get crops planted, harder to tend the animals. We don't have extra fruit and vegetables to sell. We don't have enough money to pay our property taxes. And if we can't pay, we'll be forced to sell the land." She sighed. "Gloomy times!"

"I'm sorry," said Mrs. Albright.

No wonder Raymond is miserable, thought Julie. Maybe it was because they were cousins, but it was almost as if she could feel his sadness herself.

Aunt Nadine sipped her lemonade, then smiled. "Well, it's not *all* gloom and doom! About three months ago, Vicky joined us. She used to be an accountant, and she's full of plans. It was her idea to sell our honey and bread and fresh eggs to the restaurants in town. She said we could ask the shops to sell the sweaters we knit from our own sheep's wool. Then it hit me: We'll open our *own* shop!"

Aunt Nadine stopped rocking and grabbed her sister's hand. "Joyce, you wrote about how well your shop is doing. Will you help me open a shop like Gladrags?"

Mrs. Albright smiled. "I'd be happy to."

"It will be so great to have something *good* happening here. All of us are desperate to find a way to stay. But we've had an awful run of luck. Everything we try comes to nothing. It's almost as if . . ." her voice trailed off.

"As if what?" asked Mrs. Albright.

Aunt Nadine closed her eyes. "As if . . . we're under a curse."

chapter 3

Almost Heaven

JULIE FROWNED. "WHAT kind of curse?"

Aunt Nadine rubbed her temples for a long moment, then opened her eyes. She laughed lightly. "I'm just being silly. Things will look up now that your mom's here to help." She turned to her sister. "Let's think up names for our new shop!"

Julie stood up uncertainly. "Should I find Raymond?"

"When he sinks into a mood, he usually wants me to leave him alone. But maybe you'll cheer him up!" Aunt Nadine pointed down the path. "Check the barns. That's where he'll be."

Julie left the sisters and headed for the meadow. The grass was dappled with late-afternoon light that slanted through trees. The dirt path was as wide as a city sidewalk, smoothed by many feet over the years. Silence rang in Julie's ears. She was so used to the noise of city life that the quiet was unsettling.

"Raymond?" she called, stopping at a pen outside the first barn. Inside was a large brown and white cow.

"Say hi to Mamie." Raymond appeared suddenly at her side. His eyes were red-rimmed, but he was smiling now. "And to Buttercup, her calf. Everybody's favorite baby!"

Julie reached over the fence and rubbed the cow's broad, soft head. Mamie nuzzled Julie's hand, and the calf tottered over, tail swishing. Julie rubbed Buttercup, too.

"The other cows are coming in for the night now." Raymond pointed to the meadow, where a dozen cows were being urged toward the barn by two men who clapped their hands. "Let's hurry, before they get here!" Grabbing Julie's arm,

Raymond tugged her through the wide barn door.

In the shadowy light, Julie could see a rope swing hanging from the rafters. A leather belt was looped around its seat to serve as a handle. Raymond grabbed the belt, pulling the swing behind him as he climbed up a ladder to a loft at one end of the barn, and then—*"Bombs away!"* he yelled. He leaped off the platform and soared through the air. "This is what we do for fun in the country," he called down to her.

"Wow!" Julie laughed.

When the swing came to rest and Raymond had jumped off, Julie grabbed the belt and scrambled up the ladder. She straddled the seat and pushed off. *"Bombs away!"* Her stomach swooped as the long rope sent her plunging down, down, into the barn and then up, up into the air again. Down and up, and down and up, until the swing gradually slowed and Raymond took the rope for another turn.

Raymond seemed to have tossed away his cares

while he rode the swing, but as the men reached the barn, he jumped off and ushered Julie out the side door. "We'll have to help with milking if they see us!"

Julie thought it would be fun to learn to milk a cow, but after stopping briefly to pat the sheep thronging against their pen, Raymond dashed into the second, smaller, barn. He showed her a spacious room with small tables, beanbag chairs, and low shelves of homemade wooden toys and rag dolls. "This is the playroom," he said. "And here's our schoolroom." He opened another door into a room with one big window, a round battered wooden table, and a chalkboard. "There used to be about a dozen kids, but now there's just me and Dolores—and babies too young for school. With Dolores working, she might not be back . . ." He sighed. "Then it'll just be me."

"The only kid in the whole school?" Julie marveled. "Are you in sixth grade, like me?"

Raymond shrugged. "We don't really have grades. Or teachers even. I mean, all the grown-ups take turns being our teachers for a few hours each day."

Julie had a hard time imagining such a thing.

"Come on," Raymond said. "Next stop, our beehives. Empty of bees, though."

Julie frowned. "No bees?"

"Nope. A couple of weeks ago the whole colony swarmed—that means they flew off. So now we won't have honey to sell in our new shop until we get some new bees."

Julie followed Raymond out of the barn to the edge of the woods where wooden boxes were stacked. "What made the bees leave?" she asked.

"No one knows. Loud noises . . . some kind of disturbance. Vicky thinks someone upset them on purpose, but I don't know." Raymond shrugged. "Pa can catch a swarm and lure them to the hives. I've seen him do it before! If he were here now, he'd be able to get us some new bees."

"Your dad sounds really talented with animals," said Julie. "He trains chicks and catches bees! Pretty cool."

"Pa is one cool dude," said Raymond, ducking his head so his shaggy hair hid his face. "I wish he'd move back. He practically built this place himself. He made everything work." He sighed. "My mom used to call him a jack-of-all-trades because he could build anything and fix anything. But now he says he has nothing to offer us at the ranch—just because he can't do the work he used to. He wants Ma to move into town, but she doesn't want to. She blames him for going off to war—says it ruined everything. But I don't blame him," Raymond said. "He went to Vietnam because his twin brother was a soldier who went missing in action. Pa wanted to find him."

"Did he . . . find him?" Julie ventured to ask.

"Yes—but his brother was dead." Raymond

kicked the dirt around the beehive boxes for a moment before going on. "And then my dad got wounded and came home, and nothing has been the same."

"Oh, I'm so sorry." Julie didn't know what else to say. Her cousin's sadness made her own heart ache.

"We had so much fun together," Raymond said softly. "Ma, Pa, and me. Pa always made up games. Treasure hunts. Secret codes to solve. He used to give out silly prizes. Like once he made a headband for my mom, woven out of vines and flowers. He whittled me a whole zoo of wooden animals. And he used to call me funny nicknames—anything but regular Raymond." He smiled, remembering. "Any name that started with *R*!"

Julie laughed. Uncle David sounded fun. "You mean like Ronald or Roger?"

"Yep. And Reginald, Reinhard, Raphael. At Christmas he called me Rudolph!" He kicked the dirt again, exposing something white in the dust.

"Hey," Julie said, bending down. "What's this?" She picked up a white scrap of paper. Just visible through the dust that darkened it were a sliver of a yellow sun and the last part of a word: *afe*. "Oh, it's another napkin from the Galaxy Cafe!" It was just like the one she'd found near the chicken coop.

"That's weird," Raymond said. "Maybe Vicky's right. Maybe Mr. Coker *was* here."

The shadows around the barn were deepening, and Julie couldn't help shivering and looking around worriedly, as if expecting to see the cafe owner sneaking up on them. Mr. Coker hadn't seemed like a very nice person when she'd met him at the restaurant, but she didn't like thinking he'd be mean enough to scare off the bees or let the chickens out to be killed by foxes.

"Your mom said maybe a *curse* is making things go wrong," Julie said.

Raymond shrugged. "Oh, it's just the old gold mine story."

"There's a *gold mine* here?"

Raymond was silent for a minute, as if deciding how to answer. "Yep," he said finally. "It's on our property, down by the river. Some gold miners staked claims there over a hundred years ago, but then things went wrong. The walls collapsed, and miners died. So when things go wrong at the ranch now, we say it's the miners' curse. But nobody really believes it!"

All the same, Julie thought a gold mine sounded very exciting. "I'd love to see it," she told him.

Raymond shook his head. "It's boarded up. You can go in only a few yards."

"But still—" Across the meadow, a clanging bell cut her off.

"That's the dinner bell," Raymond said. "Let's go!"

On the way back to the Big House, Julie tried to

find a way to keep the conversation about the mine going. "I saw a TV show about kids exploring an underground cave," she began.

"Lucky duck. You have TV?"

Julie stopped for a moment and stared at Raymond, forgetting about the mine for the moment. *But of course he couldn't have TV without electricity,* she realized.

"Once a year we go to Sonora for a movie on my birthday." Raymond's voice was cheerful.

No television, and a movie once a year? Julie regarded her cousin doubtfully. "We're like the city mouse and the country mouse in that old story. Our lives are so different." Julie paused. "You know that story, don't you?"

"Sure. Ma told it to me when I was little. We're not that backward out here, though."

Julie reddened. "I never said you were."

Three black-and-white dogs raced from the porch, barking, and Julie bent down to stroke them, hiding her flushed cheeks. "I think you're a lucky duck. I adore dogs, but we can't have them at our apartment."

"We have six—a whole pack," Raymond told her, cheerful again. "And three cats. Come on, I'll introduce you." He opened the screen door to the Big House.

The great room held the kitchen and dining area. Beyond that was a large living room with several battered couches and armchairs, and a stone fireplace at one end. A chess game was in progress on a coffee table and a jigsaw puzzle under construction on another table. Along one wall was an assortment of banjos, guitars, flutes—even a cello. Three cats lazed on the shabby couches. The dogs surged forward to greet Raymond and Julie.

"You get to have all these dogs," Julie marveled, accepting their licks and kisses. "*And* you only go to school for a few hours a day, *and* there's a swing in your barn, and . . . it's sort of a perfect life."

"It was when Pa lived here." Raymond's voice turned sad again.

Julie felt a little shy at meeting the ranchers, but everyone greeted her enthusiastically. There were adults and babies and toddlers all gathering around the tables in the dining area, all various ages and races. The men had long hair and bushy beards and wore overalls that looked as if they were held together with patches. Some of the women wore jeans and T-shirts; others wore flowing prairie skirts, and Rose was still in her long red caftan. Vicky, the woman with blond braids, shook Julie's hand vigorously. "You can call me Viking Vicky," she said, with a booming laugh. "Everybody does!"

"She's our self-appointed manager," Aunt Nadine told Julie with a smile. "The one I told you about with ideas for saving the ranch."

Vicky bowed low. "Fingers crossed."

Dolores was carrying a stack of plates to the table. Instead of her black and silver outfit from the cafe, she now wore jeans and a peasant blouse. "We meet again," she said. "Sorry about that order mixup today! My boss makes me nervous the way he's always hovering, like he's just waiting for me to make a mistake." Dolores seemed bubbly and at ease now that she was home, Julie noticed.

"Being a waitress looks hard," said Julie.

Rose winked at Dolores. "When we open our shop, you'll quit the cafe and work with me," she told her daughter.

The ranchers invited Julie and her mother to sit down to their simple feast of homemade cheese, whole wheat bread, potato salad, and fresh green beans. Julie sat between Dolores and Raymond.

Dolores's father, Allen, passed Julie a plate of pale yellow butter. "Churned it myself this morning," he said.

Julie spread a thick layer of butter on her bread. "Everything looks so good. I didn't think I'd ever be hungry again after that burger at the cafe!"

"So you met my daughter's boss," Rose said. "That guy would like nothing better than to fill the whole mountain with restaurants and shopping malls!"

"He did mention wanting to build a housing development here," said Mrs. Albright.

"I'll bet he did! A *luxury* housing development." Aunt Nadine sniffed. Grimly, she bit into her bread.

The ranchers asked Julie and her mom about their life in San Francisco. They wanted to hear about Mrs. Albright's shop, about Julie's sister Tracy, and about Julie's school. Raymond listened intently. *I wonder if he's lonely,* Julie thought.

Later Julie helped Aunt Nadine and Viking Vicky clear the tables, while Rose put a large pot of water onto the stove to heat. Raymond and the men went out to settle the animals for the night. After the dishes were done, Julie and her mother joined the ranchers outside.

Dusk had fallen over the mountain, and the

absence of electric lights made the stars seem brighter than they were at home. Julie plopped down next to Dolores at the edge of the porch, dangled her legs over the side, and gazed up at the stars for a long time. Some ranchers sat nearby in rocking chairs; others lay on blankets at the edge of the meadow. After a while, a bear of a man named Jet, with a thick red beard and long curls, began strumming a guitar. His young wife introduced herself as Bonnie, and she held out their baby, a chubby six-month-old named Rainbow, for Julie to cuddle while she and Jet sang a folk ballad:

Oh do you remember sweet Betsy from Pike,
Who crossed the wide prairie with her husband Ike?
With two yoke of cattle, a big yellow dog,
An old Shanghai rooster and one spotted hog . . .

Julie stroked Rainbow's silky curls. "Think of it," she said to Dolores. "Pioneer babies must have crossed the prairie just like in that song!"

"They were coming west as part of the gold rush," Dolores said. "And they settled in places just like this."

"Yeah," murmured Julie, thinking how special it would be to grow up here like baby Rainbow would—running barefoot in the meadow with the dogs, climbing trees, attending a one-room school. If Julie's friends and their families all moved to the ranch along with Julie's family, then there'd be a *ton* of kids again. Maybe Raymond would be happier. *But,* she realized, *he'd still miss his father.* And there were troubles here, Julie reminded herself, even if they seemed very far away at the moment.

"It's heavenly here," Mrs. Albright said dreamily.

Aunt Nadine grinned. "Well, we've got plenty of room for new members."

Everybody laughed. The stars winked down at them as if sharing the joke.

The night grew darker, and people began

bidding each other good night. Warm yellow lamplight glowed in the cottage windows as Julie, her mother, and Aunt Nadine strolled along the path. Back at their cottage, Julie climbed up into the loft, unrolled her sleeping bag, and curled up on the narrow cot. She could see Raymond already on the other side of the loft stretched out on his back in the dim moonlight filtering through the window.

Julie lay listening to the unfamiliar hush over the mountains, so different from the foghorns on the bay and the noisy traffic that passed outside her window in San Francisco. After what seemed like a very long time, she drifted off to sleep.

Some time later, a soft noise awoke her. In the moonlight, she saw Raymond moving to the ladder. Julie heard it creak as he climbed down, and his bare feet pad across the floor.

Then she heard the click of the front door closing.

chapter 4

Midnight in the Mine

JULIE SLID OUT of bed and peered down into the dark room. The lighted dial of her watch showed just after midnight. Where would her cousin be going at this hour?

Then she remembered the bathhouse. *Of course.* He'd be back in a minute or two.

She returned to her bed and lay back on the pillow, thinking about how, in winter, a trip to the bathhouse would mean heading out into the snow. Her ears strained in the darkness, listening for the cottage door to open again, but it didn't. Where *was* Raymond?

She wondered whether she should alert Aunt Nadine. Maybe Raymond was sick. She slipped out of bed and went to the small window. She looked outside, hoping to spot the gleam of her cousin's flashlight. She saw nothing. Was he sitting on the porch?

Quiet as a mouse—a city mouse—Julie climbed down the ladder. Tiptoeing past her mom on the couch, Julie opened the front door. The porch was empty. But wait, there *was* a light! There—at the edge of the trees. And again, moving deeper into the woods.

Julie slid her feet into her sandals and closed the door softly behind her. Quietly, she followed the path to the edge of the woods, wishing she also had a flashlight. The air was warm and scented with pine, and the moon was bright and lit the path, but as soon as she stepped into the woods, the night grew much darker. "Raymond?" she called softly.

Immediately she heard a rustling noise farther up the path, and then he was there, shining his flashlight in her face. She raised her hands to shield her eyes.

"Cripes!" he hissed at her. "What are you doing out here?"

"I was worried, and then I saw your flash-light . . ."

"So you just thought you'd *follow* me?" Raymond glared at her.

Well, you're my cousin, she thought.

But before she could reply he clicked off his light abruptly. "Shhhh!" They stood in darkness.

"What is it?" she whispered.

Raymond remained still for a long moment, as if deciding whether to answer. Then, without a word, he moved through the trees. His feet were silent on the path.

Julie could hear the rushing sound of water, and soon saw the dark ribbon of water cutting deeply through the riverbank. Under the cover of the sound of the river, Raymond spoke in a low voice. "I saw lights in the woods the other night, but when I started to follow them, they disappeared." He edged along a narrower path to the left, away from the river, and Julie followed close behind. "So when I saw them again tonight, I just had to follow." He stopped suddenly. In front of them jutted a rocky ledge. "See, up ahead? I think they're at the mine."

Julie stared into the darkness ahead. She saw a flicker of light, then another, then nothing.

Raymond moved forward without making a sound. He didn't seem the least bit scared to be out here in the woods at night, but Julie was. She followed, holding her breath.

Raymond moved around an outcropping of rock and stopped. "There," he whispered.

"Where?" A deep shadow opened between the rocks in front of them. "Is it a *cave*?" whispered Julie. There were no lights anywhere.

"It starts out as a cave, but it's the gold mine I told you about." Raymond ducked his head and entered the mouth of the cave. "The miners dug deep down into the mountain."

Julie stepped inside. The air smelled of wet earth.

Raymond clicked on his flashlight and directed the beam at the back of the cave. Then he spoke in his normal voice, not bothering to whisper. "You can only walk so far, and then it's boarded up." He shook his head, looking puzzled. "I was sure this is where the lights were headed, but nobody's in here. It's weird." He shot the beam of light to illuminate the back of the natural cave about fifteen feet in. Old boards were nailed across an opening, beyond which there was only blackness.

"Those boards cover a tunnel the miners dug ages ago," Raymond said.

Julie peered over the barricade. "I don't see anything."

Raymond's flashlight flickered, and he shut it off again. "I need new batteries," he muttered.

Complete darkness engulfed them, and Julie felt dizzy. She reached out to the top board to steady herself and felt it shift under her hand. "Whoa," she whispered. "Turn your light back on!"

Raymond clicked it on.

"Shine it right here, on this top board."

He directed the dim beam onto the barricade. The top board was fastened across the opening to the tunnel with rusty nails. But when Julie jiggled it, she found she could raise it easily.

Raymond laid the flashlight on the rocky ledge at the side of the barricade, and together they discovered they could lift the board right off the old nails. The next board lifted off just as easily. The rest of the barricade was securely in place, but with the top two boards removed, it would be easy enough to climb over into the tunnel.

Julie gazed into the silent darkness beyond the barricade. How far did it go? And where? Excitement tingled along her shoulders.

Raymond directed his light into the tunnel. The waning beam showed a passage about six feet high and four feet wide, stretching a short distance, then curving to the left. "Whoever had the light could have gone in there. We could go in, too."

Julie hesitated. "If someone is coming here in the middle of the night, they probably don't want anyone to know."

Raymond looked thoughtful. "And that's weird," he said. "Anybody from the ranch wouldn't need to sneak in here. So . . . whoever has been going in there is trespassing. But why?"

"What could they be looking for?" Julie wondered.

Then they both looked at each other and said at the same time: "Gold!"

Raymond's flashlight died completely, and he nearly tripped over the boards they'd stacked on the ground. "We can't go inside without light," he whispered.

"No," Julie agreed with a shiver, and she wasn't at all sorry.

Feeling their way, they settled the two boards back into place. They left the cave and followed the narrow path along the river. Without the flashlight's beam to guide them, Julie felt disoriented by the river rushing below them. She grabbed the back of Raymond's pajama shirt and didn't let it go until the path turned uphill toward the moonlit meadow.

Raymond stopped at the edge of the woods. "If there's gold in there, it belongs to the ranch. It could pay the taxes. I don't want someone stealing it!"

"So . . . we need to tell your mom," said Julie.

"No," said Raymond. "Don't tell anybody just yet. If there is any gold, I'm going to find it myself. For once, I'd like Ma to have a *good* surprise."

Though she could not see his face, Julie could feel his determination. Finding gold seemed like a long shot, like the kind of thing that only happened in movies. Still, it was nice to hear her cousin sound so positive.

"Okay, then," she said. "I'll help."

chapter 5

Cousins United

"RISE AND SHINE, sleepyhead!" Aunt Nadine called, standing on the ladder and poking her head up where Julie could see her. "Raymond's been up since the crack of dawn doing his chores, and your mom went to breakfast ages ago."

Julie blinked in the soft sunlight shining through the loft window. She never slept so late at home! She dressed quickly and dashed out the door toward the bathhouse.

By the time she arrived at the Big House, three of the long tables were already scrubbed clean. The fourth table was still set for breakfast, with a pot of oatmeal, a jug of fresh milk, and a bowl of blackberries. Mrs. Albright sat at one end with Viking Vicky, deep in conversation. Vicky, her yellow braids piled high, was writing in a spiral notebook. Dolores and her mother, Rose, stood at the other end of the table, chopping onions and carrots.

When Mrs. Albright saw Julie, she broke off her conversation with a smile. "Good morning! Vicky and I are making plans for the new shop. Come try these blackberries! I picked them myself."

Julie pulled out a chair next to her mom and reached for a plump blackberry. "I'm glad there's some left! Everyone's up so early here."

"There's tons to do around here," Dolores said. "So we're all up with the sun."

"Every day, there are cows to milk, animals to feed, and pens to clean," Rose said with a smile. "There are eggs to gather, butter to churn, and gardens to weed. Today is laundry day, so that's an extra ton of work. We're heating water now for the washtubs. Once everything is washed, we'll hang the wet laundry out on the lines to dry."

Julie blinked at all this information and stirred

her oatmeal. At home, her morning chores were making her bed and wiping the sink clean after she'd brushed her teeth. Laundry was done easily in the machines in the basement of her apartment building.

"Raymond is gathering the eggs," said Aunt Nadine. "When he's done, he'll show you the rest of our ranch."

"Wish I could come, too," said Dolores, "but I've got to get to the cafe." With a wave, she was gone, the screen door banging behind her.

Raymond appeared with a basket of eggs just as Julie was carrying her dishes to the sink. Jet, the man who had played guitar the night before, came in next with a basket of ripe tomatoes, and handed them to Aunt Nadine to wash under the pump at the sink. "I can make a great sauce with these," she said.

"I can help," Julie said.

"Not this time," said Rose. "Raymond, you

give Julie the full tour. We want her to feel at home while she's here!"

Vicky looked up from her notebook. "But keep well away from the old mine."

"There's nothing to worry about," said Aunt Nadine. "David boarded it up years ago."

"Oh, but wouldn't it be cool if you could still go in?" Julie couldn't help taking the opportunity to probe. "What if there was still some gold left in there?"

Raymond shot her a warning look, but she wasn't going to say anything about their midnight adventure. She smiled innocently at him.

Rose shook her head. "You'd have to time-travel back a hundred and twenty-five years to find any gold in there. Back then, this mountain was crowded with people panning for gold in the river, trying to strike it rich."

Julie's heart gave a little jump. "The miners found gold just lying in the water?"

"Practically!" Rose's smile flashed. "The miners would squat by the river and scoop up dirt into a pan and then add water, shaking the pan so the heavy gold particles sank to the bottom. They did it all day!"

"It was intense work," Aunt Nadine added. "And as time passed, gold became even harder to find. That's when the miners started digging into the mountains near the rivers. Imagine how hard that would have been without machines!"

Jet put his hands on his hips. "Those miners had a hard time—but they caused a lot of trouble, too. They came to this beautiful land, and the first thing they did was start cutting down ancient trees and hunting all the animals. The gold's all gone now, and because of them, wolves and bears are extinct in California, too. It's easy to forget the damage those miners did."

"Oh, don't lecture the kids," Rose said mildly.

Jet's laugh rumbled through the kitchen. "I don't

mean to preach, but it's important to remember that the miners left a legacy they didn't intend. Most of them only wanted to get rich quick—just like the developers who want our land now."

"In fact," Aunt Nadine cut in, "we're related to one of those greedy old miners. Raymond's great-great-grandfather, Joaquin Sandoval—on his pa's side of the family—had what they called 'gold fever.' The story goes that he found a lot of gold. Then he went off to San Francisco to build a mansion. He never came back to his wife and baby. Talk about a bad legacy." Aunt Nadine shook her head.

Jet smiled. "Good thing we ranchers are different. We take care of nature here, just as it takes care of us. We don't take too much from the land, and we don't build grand mansions."

"Oh, yes we do!" Rose said with a wink. "I'd say our tree house is pretty grand."

"A tree house!" Julie grinned.

"Raymond can show it to you on your tour,"

Aunt Nadine said. "He built it himself."

"*Pa* built it," Raymond corrected her. "I just helped."

Aunt Nadine sighed. "Come back in time for lunch, kids. Have fun."

Raymond grabbed a handful of blackberries from the bowl and headed outside. Julie followed him past the barns to the same path they'd used the previous night. Now sunlight spilled through the trees. Insects hummed and birds sang overhead.

The path curved to meet the river, which rushed between steep banks that were studded with small trees, many with exposed roots where erosion had washed away the soil over time. Julie imagined miners crouched at the edges of the river, picking flakes of gold from their pans. Rose said the gold was long gone, but Julie couldn't help scanning the riverbank as they walked, alert for any gleam of forgotten gold. Just as she was scolding herself for being so silly, a glint of something caught her eye.

She stopped and peered more closely into the tangle of roots at the base of an oak tree that was growing out of the riverbank. "Hey, look," she called to her cousin.

"What?" asked Raymond. "I don't see anything."

"There, in the tree roots." Julie scrambled down the riverbank onto a flat, ivy-covered outcropping of rock a few feet above the water and examined the knot of roots growing out from the bank next to the rock. A glint of glass caught the light. Julie bent to scrape at the dirt, revealing a small bottle stuck in the roots. She broke off a stick from an overhanging branch and used it to pry the bottle the rest of the way out.

The little red flask fit neatly in the palm of her hand. It was streaked with dirt, but unbroken. It had a short neck and clear glass stopper. Gently, Julie tugged at the stopper, but it didn't budge. Maybe if she rinsed it? Julie knelt by the river and swished the bottle in the water, scraping at the dirt with her fingernails, then held the bottle up to the sunlight. The glass gleamed like fire, and she saw now that the stopper was sealed with some sort of glue.

She clambered up the riverbank and held the bottle out to Raymond. "I think it's a perfume bottle," Julie said. She thought of Dolores's soft flowery scent and how Aunt Nadine smelled of lemon. "Maybe one of the ranchers lost it?"

"Who carries perfume on a hike?"

Julie had to admit it didn't make much sense. Could the bottle have been dropped by whoever had been sneaking into the mine?

That made even less sense.

"Come on." Raymond waved to her from farther up the path. "It's just an old bottle."

Julie slipped the bottle into the pocket of her shorts and set off after Raymond. She'd open the bottle later. Maybe there was still some perfume inside.

Raymond strode ahead on the path that twisted and turned through the woods to a clearing.

"Whoa!" cried Julie, gazing up. Rope bridges connected three gnarled old oak trees. A tall wooden tower rose up from the middle tree. "It's a storybook palace!"

"Welcome to the Gold Moon tree house," Raymond said with quiet pride. "It was Pa's own design . . ." His voice trailed off, and he made a sweeping gesture with his arm. "I don't come here that much anymore. I mean, with all the kids gone, it's like a ghost town now."

Hoping to lighten Raymond's mood, Julie reached out and playfully tapped him on the shoulder. "Well, too bad those other kids aren't here to help you now," she said with a grin. "Because . . . you're IT!" She jumped away and ran to the first ladder.

With a happy shout he chased her, and they spent the next hour climbing high among the branches, swinging down on knotted ropes, racing across the bridges, and finally collapsing inside the tower to catch their breath.

In the distance the lunch bell clanged. "Truce?" yelled Raymond.

Julie admired how deftly he swung down from the tree-house tower, like some jungle monkey. She had to go more slowly, hanging on tightly to the knotted rope, but soon stood safely beside him.

"Pretty good, for a city mouse," he said with a smirk. Julie felt a glow of pleasure at her cousin's teasing.

They walked back along the trail side by side. The water surged over the rocks, splashing up against the sides of the steep riverbank. Remembering the bottle she'd found, Julie slipped her hand into her pocket and rubbed her fingers on its cool, hard glass. She wondered whose hands had held it before hers.

chapter 6
More Trouble

BACK AT THE Big House, Julie and Raymond found a pot of vegetable soup simmering on the stove. Aunt Nadine slid four loaves of crusty bread from the oven. The ranchers gathered at the long tables to gobble soup and fresh bread.

"The mountain air agrees with you," said Aunt Nadine, leaning over to pour Julie some milk. She set down the milk pitcher and clapped her hands. "Okay," she said, "what'll it be first, ladies? Learn to spin and weave—or milk a cow?"

"I'd love to see your weaving room," said Julie's mom. Julie would rather have learned to milk a cow. But after lunch Aunt Nadine linked her arms through Julie's and Mrs. Albright's, and they all walked together to the sheep enclosure.

"These fluffy fellows are the source of our Gold Moon Ranch hand-knit sweaters," Aunt Nadine told them proudly. "David gave me four lambs as a wedding present. Now there's a whole flock."

Julie tried to pat one of the soft white sheep, but it skittered out of her reach.

"They're shy," Aunt Nadine said with a laugh. "Keep trying. When they're used to you, they'll start following you around!" She then explained how their wool was shorn, carded, soaked, spun into yarn, and then given soft colors with vegetable and bark dyes.

"Now come see our weaving room." Aunt Nadine led Julie and Mrs. Albright into an airy space where Viking Vicky was rolling yarn into tight balls of wool.

"These are the looms and spinning wheels we use for the wool." Vicky pointed to the large, old-fashioned contraptions standing by the windows. "Let me show you how they work."

Fascinated, Julie tried her hand at the big old spinning wheel, thrilling at the way the springy mass of wool pulled tight in her fingers and spun out into a thin, strong length of yarn.

Mrs. Albright sat down with Viking Vicky and began discussing selling homemade sweaters at Gladrags. Julie peeked into the laundry room, where Bonnie was lifting the wet clothing out of a deep tub and her husband, Jet, was turning a hand crank that ran the clothes through a set of rollers to squeeze it dry.

"Come to lend a hand?" asked Jet, pushing his long red curls off his forehead.

"Sure, if you show me what to do," Julie replied.

Julie helped peg all the heavy, wet laundry on the long clotheslines behind the vegetable gardens. It was hot, tiring work, and by the time they'd finished, Julie was surprised to find it was late afternoon. Time seemed to pass so quickly here at the commune. *Because the work never stops,* she realized.

"We got a late start, so the clothes might not have time to dry," Bonnie said as they carried the empty baskets back to the laundry room. "We may have to leave everything overnight and let the morning sun finish it off."

"I'll help with folding," Julie promised.

Julie accompanied her mother and aunt back to the Big House, where Rose was setting up an assembly line to make chili. Aunt Nadine, Julie's mom, and others set to work pounding fresh tomatoes into a sauce, chopping herbs, and mixing up batter for corn bread. Soon, the tang of garlic hung in the air and Julie's mouth watered.

Rose handed Julie a basket of cutlery. "Will you help me set the tables?" she asked, adding, "I wish Dolores didn't work such long hours. I miss her help here at home."

As Julie set spoons and forks on the tables, she felt ashamed to think of how often she and Tracy grumbled at having to set the table or vacuum their apartment. "Does Dolores come home for dinner?" she asked.

"She gets here when she gets here," said Rose. "It's a long walk up the mountain."

A car engine broke the quiet. Julie followed Allen out to the porch in time to watch a long, low sports car crunch up the gravel drive. "It's Coker," Allen growled, starting down to the parking area. "What can he want now?" Julie watched as Dolores climbed out of the car. Mr. Coker, looking overdressed in his jacket and tie, was smiling and trying to talk to Allen, but Allen's arms were crossed and he was shaking his head.

Dolores walked up the path to the Big House and waved to Julie. "Dad isn't very happy that I got a ride home from the enemy," she said. "But I cut my hand at work, and Mr. Coker helped me bandage it."

"Oh dear," said Rose. "Let me see!"

Dolores waved her mother away. "It isn't bad.

Doesn't need stitches. But boy, those knives are sharp! They can cut through anything, Mr. Coker says."

"That man," said a voice behind them. Both girls turned to see Viking Vicky at the door with a worried look on her pretty face. "He shouldn't be here."

"It was good of him to help Dolores," said Rose. "And it's good of him to hire her in the first place."

"Yes, of course, but he's just trying to butter her up so we'll sell the land to him."

Julie was perplexed. "But didn't you say he's the one messing things up around here?"

"Yes," Vicky said firmly. "It makes perfect sense: He wants to make life hard for us so we'll decide we need to sell our land. Yet he wants to seem friendly so we'll turn to him when we decide to leave." She turned to Dolores. "Don't let your guard down around that man."

"I'm glad you're okay," Rose said soothingly.

She put her arm around her daughter's shoulders. "Come have dinner."

"I'll wash up and be right there," Dolores said. Then she hurried down the path toward the bathhouse.

After dinner, the ranchers headed out to the meadow with their guitars and tambourines. The evening breeze rustled through the trees. Soft voices rose in the evening air as darkness crept over the mountains.

Michael, row the boat ashore, alleluia!

Julie marveled at the way Raymond and Dolores harmonized. At home, she realized, her family never sang together. Could she harmonize with Tracy? They'd never tried. Maybe these things came with practice.

"I love it here," she said to Dolores and Raymond. "You guys are so lucky."

Dolores reached out and squeezed Julie's hand with her unbandaged one. She leaned close, and her dark hair brushed against Julie's blond braid. Her faint flowery scent reminded Julie of the bottle from the riverbank.

"I like your perfume," Julie said.

Dolores looked pleased. "It's just cheap stuff from the drugstore in town," she said. "My parents always say fresh mountain air is the nicest scent, but sometimes I like things from the modern world! The tourists who come to the cafe always have the coolest clothes. The girls wear makeup. And the kids have transistor radios with all the latest music. You're a taste of the modern world yourself, Julie, coming from the big city. I bet you have your own transistor radio . . ."

"And a TV set right in your living room!" Raymond interjected.

Julie grinned. "I do have my own radio," she said. "And we do have a TV in our living room."

"Do you watch soap operas?" asked Dolores eagerly. "Sometimes I watch them when I visit my aunt and uncle in town. I'd love to write one myself and see it on TV someday!"

"Dolores is always writing," Raymond said. "Stories and poems and stuff."

"Not so much any more." Dolores sighed, leaning back on the blanket. "Work takes up so much time."

Bonnie walked over to them, with Rainbow on her hip. "Would you kids keep an eye on Rainbow while I check the laundry?" Bonnie deposited the baby in Julie's lap. "If the clothes are dry, we'll take them down before the dew gets everything damp all over again."

"Of course!" Julie grinned at the baby. "Hi, little one. What song should we sing next?"

Rainbow chortled and reached out to pull Julie's long braid.

"This Land Is Your Land!" Raymond called out.

Jet nodded his bushy red head and started strumming the chords.

Julie was trying to harmonize with Dolores when a ragged shout made them both jump.

"Oh no!" Bonnie stood at the edge of the meadow, waving her arms. "I could use some help here!"

The singing broke off. "What is it?" Julie cried. She scrambled to her feet.

Raymond got up slowly, frowning. Jet set down his guitar and reached for the baby. Carrying Rainbow in his strong arms, he strode across the meadow. Julie ran after him, with Raymond and Dolores right behind.

chapter 7

A Lad Strong and Bold

THE RANCHERS STARED at the clothing, sheets, and towels that had been hung carefully out on the lines earlier, all now lying in the dirt.

Bonnie clutched her head. "Hours wasted . . . hours and hours." Her voice trembled. "This is awful!"

Julie picked up a shirt and tried to shake it clean. The laundry, still damp, was rumpled and dirt-streaked, and it would all have to be washed again by hand, wrung out, and hung up to dry. Julie felt tired just thinking about all that work.

"Could the cows have knocked down the lines?" Mrs. Albright asked.

"No, the posts are still standing." Allen gestured to the wooden poles that held up the lines.

They stood tall and firm. "It's just the lines that are broken. Cows couldn't do that."

"It's the curse," said Aunt Nadine, half laughing, half crying.

"Pa could fix the lines in no time," Raymond said. "He can fix anything."

Aunt Nadine closed her eyes briefly, then opened them. "Raymond, honey," she said.

Then Allen let out an angry bellow. "Look here!" He brandished the end of a laundry line. "This rope didn't just *unravel*. Someone *deliberately* cut the lines."

Jet snatched up another laundry line. "Sure enough," he muttered. "Sliced right in two."

"Who would do such a thing?" asked Mrs. Albright.

"Eli Coker, maybe?" said Viking Vicky grimly. The setting sun glinted on her crown of braids.

"But Mr. Coker isn't even here," Julie pointed out.

"But remember who brought Dolores home," her mother said slowly, and Julie nodded. *Eli Coker.*

"Did anyone actually *see* him leave?" Vicky asked.

Rose looked thoughtful. "We all came in for dinner. He could have parked down the drive just out of sight and walked back up here."

Everyone grumbled about the endless work. What a lot of bother even to heat the water again! And the sky looked like rain. As much as the ranchers welcomed late summer rain after the long dry season, it would be that much harder to dry the laundry.

Julie helped bundle the soiled clothing into baskets, thoughts tumbling in her head. Mr. Coker must have plenty of sharp knives at the cafe. He could have brought one here to cut the lines.

But it seemed like something a mean kid might do, not a grown-up.

Julie shook her head, feeling disloyal at the turn

her thoughts were taking. Dolores and Raymond were the only kids on the ranch big enough to cut the lines, but that would mean . . . She glanced at the older girl, who was stuffing dirt-streaked sheets into a wicker basket.

Dolores glanced up as if she'd felt Julie's gaze. "It's awful, isn't it?" she said.

"I know," said Julie, flushing. "That's what I was just thinking."

Dolores tossed back her dark cloud of hair and lifted the heavy laundry basket. "I hope we catch him in the act next time," she said.

"So you think it's Mr. Coker who did this?"

"Who else?" Dolores asked. She lifted the basket and carted it off to the laundry room in the barn.

Who else indeed? Julie lifted her basket of clothing and followed slowly. She remembered the napkins they'd found by the chicken coop and the beehives. Dolores herself could have brought them home from the cafe. Julie had seen how critical Mr. Coker was of Dolores. Could Dolores be trying to get back at him by making everyone think he was causing trouble at the ranch?

The evening of singing under the stars was ruined. After gathering the laundry, the ranchers hurried off to their cottages. Julie felt troubled as Dolores hugged her good night, holding her bandaged hand out so it wouldn't get bumped, her flowery scent soft in the night air.

In the bathhouse Julie used the unfamiliar pit toilet, then stood at the sink, lit overhead by a battery-operated lamp. She stared into the mirror at her sunburned cheeks and windblown hair, thinking she was starting to look like a rancher after only one day. She slipped the perfume bottle from her pocket and held it to her nose. Was there a faint scent of flowers?

Raymond came into the bathhouse and went

straight to the pump. He pumped vigorously and bent his head for a long drink of water.

"Maybe this bottle belonged to Dolores," Julie said to him. "Maybe she lost it when she was walking by the river."

"Maybe," he said, wiping his mouth with the back of his hand.

"Where would she have been going—toward the mine?" Julie's voice was thoughtful. An idea was starting to form, and, like the thought that Dolores could have cut the laundry lines, it made her uncomfortable.

Dolores, she reasoned, wanted money for the ranch as much as Raymond did. As much as any of the ranchers did. "Maybe Dolores went to the mine last night. Maybe she was the person with the flashlight in the woods."

Raymond stared at her. "You think Dolores is after the gold?"

"Well, she could be, right? She wears perfume.

She might have been coming back from the mine in the dark at some point and didn't notice she'd dropped the bottle." Even as she said this, Julie felt unsure. The bottle seemed as though it had been stuck in the roots for a pretty long time.

She held the bottle to the light and studied it. It was hard to see anything inside the deep ruby glass, but there seemed to be a shadow. She shook the bottle. "I think there's something inside!" She scraped the glue with her fingernail. It was soft and crumbly.

"Let me see!" Raymond inspected the bottle. "Hey, it's not glue holding the stopper in. It's wax!"

"Wax?" Julie's nail scissors were in her suitcase in the cottage. They would scrape away the wax.

"Let's open it!" Raymond clicked off the lamp. "Maybe there's gold inside."

Julie laughed. "You have gold on the brain."

Together they ran to the cottage and scrambled up the ladder to the loft. Julie knelt by her suitcase and rummaged around for her little bag of toiletries. She scraped at the wax with her nail scissors, and in another minute the clear glass stopper, fitted with a cork, popped out in her hand.

She held the bottle to her nose and sniffed. The faintest scent of jasmine, like a wisp of a ghost, wafted into the room. She tipped the bottle and shook it, but whatever was inside did not come out. It looked like a tightly rolled scroll of paper.

"It's not gold," Julie announced.

"But maybe it's some kind of map to the gold?" Raymond moved closer. From the pocket of his jeans he pulled out a small Swiss army knife. "Pa gave me this for my birthday. It's got knife blades and a screwdriver and—" He slid out a thin pair of tweezers. "Try these."

"Perfect!" Using the tweezers, Julie teased a tiny scroll of paper out of the bottle into her palm. She unrolled it carefully.

Julie held the scrap of paper to the lamplight.

One side was uneven and ragged, as if it had been torn from a larger piece. Julie puzzled over the unfamiliar cursive script. The first two lines were in bold, black pencil, and seemed to be the start of a poem. But the rest of the message, still in the same spidery handwriting, looked as if hastily scratched:

There once was a lad strong and bold
Who left home to find pots of gold—

No, darling girl, no time for a poem.
Just me, saying I'm sorry for my one last hurrah.
I meant to bring you perfume in this bottle,
but now it carries a message instead.
God only knows if you'll receive it.
You were right all along.
Love's already made me rich.
If I ever get out, I'm coming home.

Yours eternally, Jack

Julie was intrigued. There seemed to be a larger story behind this note. "Who is Jack, and why did he write this?" she murmured. "Who is his 'darling girl?' And what's 'one last hurrah'?"

"Who cares?" Raymond folded his penknife and shoved it into his pocket. "It isn't a map." He looked out the window.

Julie read the message again. "You said that Dolores likes to write. Could it be a story of hers?"

Raymond leaned over the note. "That doesn't look like her handwriting. And the words don't sound like her. They don't even make sense." He snapped his fingers. "Maybe it's some kind of code! It could help us after all!"

"What do you mean?"

"There once was a lad strong and bold," he quoted from the paper. *"Who left home to find pots of gold—* that could be a code telling where a miner buried his stash of gold."

"Buried gold sounds like pirates, not miners."

Julie shook her head. "It sounds more like a love letter. Does Dolores have a boyfriend? Maybe he wrote this."

Raymond looked skeptical. "I suppose she could have met someone in town. But she's never mentioned anyone."

"Right," Julie said, disappointed. Still, boyfriend or no, it didn't mean Dolores hadn't been to the mine.

"Shh," Raymond added, looking out the window again. "Here come our moms."

They fell silent as they heard the sisters come into the cottage. Raymond lay on his bed, gesturing with his own brand of sign language that Julie understood to mean *When they're sleeping, we'll go back to the mine!*

Nodding, she slid into her sleeping bag. She tucked the little bottle and its message under her pillow, wondering whether Dolores was also tucked into bed, waiting for her parents to fall asleep so she could sneak out to the mine. Were they all looking for gold for the same reason, Julie wondered. To save the ranch? Or was Dolores searching for another reason—a reason she needed to keep secret?

Maybe she just wants money to buy her own transistor radio and a TV, Julie thought as she drifted to sleep.

The moon was high in the sky, nearly covered by clouds, when Raymond poked Julie awake. Silently, they crept down the ladder into the living room and slipped on their shoes. Raymond lifted two flashlights from the hook by the door and handed one to Julie.

Outside they tested the lights to be sure the beams were strong. "New batteries," whispered Raymond. "Keep your light off until we're in the woods."

Julie nodded, and they set off, following the path behind the barns and into the woods. After switching on their flashlights, they walked toward the river along the rutted path. A light rain had begun to fall, and the river sounded louder than it had before. Julie swept her light along the riverbank, looking for the gleam of other hidden glass bottles. But there was nothing.

The entrance to the cave lay in shadow. Julie and Raymond slipped in and, just as before, the wooden boards nailed across the entrance lifted off easily. They each removed a board and leaned it at the side of the cave.

As she climbed over the remaining boards into the mine, Julie reached up and touched the old ceiling beams, thinking about the miners who had stepped just where she was stepping, having come through this same entrance so many years ago. The wooden beams were dark with age. "What if the whole roof caves in on us?" she whispered.

"We won't go far," Raymond assured her. "Let's just see what's around that bend."

Reluctantly, Julie followed him. "Okay, but no farther!"

The tunnel felt much cooler than the night outside. The passage was about four feet wide and just her height, though at some places she needed to duck to avoid bumping her head on the wooden beams.

After a few steps, Julie froze. She reached out a hand and grabbed Raymond's arm. "Do you hear that?"

In the distance, a muffled tapping sound started and stopped and started again. Was it the sound of digging?

"Dolores?" Raymond called.

They stood, listening.

"It's stopped now," said Julie.

They clicked off their flashlights. They stood stock still, the heavy darkness closing around them like a shroud. Julie felt as if she were in the center of the earth. She closed her eyes, and it was the same as with them wide open.

A vision of a ghostly miner digging with a pickaxe into the hard earth of the mountain moved behind Julie's closed eyes. When she opened her eyes again, she was relieved to see the beam of Raymond's flashlight bobbing just ahead. He went around the bend in the passage, and she darted after him.

Immediately around the bend, they stopped. The corridor ended at a wall of dirt packed between wooden beams much like the ones overhead. To the left was an avalanche of earth, the site of a collapsed ceiling. To the right, the passage narrowed, then opened into a room about as big as the cottage living room, but with a much lower ceiling. If Julie were any taller, she would need to duck her head.

Julie and Raymond played their lights around the room. In one corner, a pickaxe leaned against the wall. Next to it lay an iron hammer and a coil of half-rotted rope. A battered lantern hung on an iron hook fixed into the wall. "These things look ancient," Julie whispered.

Raymond lifted the old lantern off the hook, and shook it. "There's no kerosene in it," he whispered. "This isn't what caused the lights I saw."

"We'd better go—" Julie broke off in midsentence. The sound had started again, clearly coming from behind the collapsed mound of earth to the left: *tap, tap, tap.*

How could anyone be behind the collapsed tunnel wall? Julie and Raymond stared at each other. Suddenly the idea of ghostly miners didn't seem so impossible.

They fairly flew down the passage, climbed out into the cave, and, with shaking hands, replaced the boards before dashing outside. The cool drizzle of rain on their faces was soothing.

A coyote howled in the rain as they ran along

the trail, flashlights bobbing. *There must be an explanation for the tapping,* Julie thought. *There must be!*

She slowed when her light bounced off something white at the side of the trail. *Not another napkin from the Galaxy cafe!* she thought, turning her light onto the object. It wasn't a paper napkin. It was a cotton handkerchief like the kind her father always kept folded in his shirt pocket. And the spots of color on it were not a printed rocket flying to the sun. Julie picked up the handkerchief and squinted in the dim light. The spots looked like smears of blood.

Julie's heart thumped hard. "Raymond!" Her voice was loud, and a rustling sound in the trees let her know it had disturbed the birds or other creatures living there.

Raymond's light bobbed back toward her. "What is it?"

Julie held out the handkerchief. "There's blood on it!"

"Are you hurt?" asked Raymond.

"No. It was here at the side of the trail." Uneasily Julie looked around. "Remember? Dolores cut her hand—maybe the cut opened up again if she was digging."

"But she couldn't have gotten in there to dig. The boards were up," Raymond pointed out.

"Still, she could be hurt. Should we check if she's okay?" Julie turned to go back.

"She's obviously already gone ahead of us. She'll be at her cottage by now. If it *is* her." Raymond began walking again, and Julie followed. When they emerged from the woods they ran through the rain back to the cottage. Quietly, they climbed up into the loft and crawled, damp and chilled, into their beds.

"I'm going back tomorrow," Raymond whispered across the room. "I'll do my chores extra fast and go before lunch. Maybe you can distract everyone from wondering where I am . . ." His voice broke off into a wide yawn that made Julie yawn, too. She curled up in her sleeping bag and listened to the gentle patter of rain on the cottage roof. It was such an unusual sound in summertime. The *tap, tap* of raindrops reminded her of the *tap, tap, tap* they'd heard in the mine.

Soon she heard Raymond's steady breathing. She felt under her pillow for the little bottle and was soon asleep herself, holding it in her hand like a talisman.

chapter 8

No Time for a Poem

JULIE WOKE TO a clear, pine-scented morning. Across the loft, she could see Raymond's empty bed, the sheet pulled up neatly. Julie dressed in a T-shirt and shorts, tucked the red bottle into her pocket, then climbed down from the loft to discover that her mom and Aunt Nadine were also gone.

She walked to the Big House, where Mrs. Albright, Aunt Nadine, Rose, and Dolores called good morning from the front porch. Julie noticed that the older girl's bandaged hand did not stop her from holding a fork and eating a plateful of scrambled eggs.

"Raymond helped the men get the clotheslines back up," Aunt Nadine told Julie. "Now he's doing his other chores."

"Help yourself to breakfast," Rose said. "I made an omelet. There's some on the stove."

Julie loaded up a plate with eggs and a slice of bread and jam. When she returned to the porch, Dolores moved over to make room on the top step.

"Do you work today?" Julie asked her.

"Not until lunch," Dolores said. "It's nice to have the morning off."

Was Dolores planning to look for gold on her free morning? Julie reached out to stroke the furry head of one of the border collies, wondering how to distract Dolores to give Raymond time to explore the mine himself. The dog pressed his head against Julie's leg, and she rubbed his ears.

"He likes you," Dolores said. "He could be yours for keeps if you moved here."

Julie thought about their apartment in San Francisco, and her dad's house, and her school. "It's so beautiful here, but there'd be things I'd miss," she admitted. "Like my friends."

"Yeah." Dolores's voice was wistful.

"And I love being able to go to the library after school, and shopping on weekends."

"Shopping! You don't know how lucky you are! I dream of big-city department stores." Dolores's eyes shone. "And a big-city library? I'd love to have one around here. Sonora's library is so small, and I've read everything in our ranch library at *least* a dozen times! Even the boring books!"

"Wait. You have a library here?" asked Julie in surprise. "Will you show me?" *That will keep Dolores busy for a little while,* Julie thought.

"Sure!" Dolores jumped up from the steps. "Not much to see, though." As she put out a hand to pull Julie up, Julie could smell the faint, flowery scent of Dolores's perfume. Was it the same as the scent in the bottle?

They stepped back inside the Big House and slid their dishes into the pan of sudsy water. Dolores led Julie down the hall to a small room with a few bookshelves and a sagging couch. Julie scanned the shelves. There were some stacks of *National Geographic* magazines, a basket of picture books for little kids, and a shelf of paperbacks. On the bottom shelf were cookbooks and gardening manuals. Dolores pointed to two cardboard boxes stacked in the corner. "I found those books out in the barn last month. I brought them in here because, well, I'll read any books I can get my hands on! But they're pretty boring. I like mysteries and romance! The weird thing is that nobody here knows who they belong to or how they got in the barn."

Julie went over to the top box and picked out a book. *Resort Management*, it was titled. The next book was called *Getting Started in the Hotel Business*. Inside on the first page, the name *Alma V. King* was written in bold, flowing script. Julie didn't remember meeting anybody with that name. Probably a rancher who'd moved away had left the books behind. But then why didn't anybody recognize the name?

Dolores pointed to an empty bookcase. "That used to be full of games, too. But the families who left took them away with them. And that top shelf? It used to be full of David's poetry books, but he took them when he left. David adores writing poetry. Sometimes he used to make treasure hunts for all us kids with little rhyming clues."

"What kind of treasure would you find at the end?" Julie asked, eager to know more about the uncle she'd never met.

"Freshly baked cookies or fresh hot doughnuts!" Dolores bit her lower lip. "I miss David."

Julie had been on a scavenger hunt at a birthday party once, but no one had ever planned a treasure hunt for her. "I want to meet David," she said. "He sounds really cool."

"He is," Dolores said. "Everybody here hopes he and Nadine will work things out. I wish he'd come back to the ranch, even if he can't do the work he used to do. He could just—oh, I don't know—sit around writing poetry if he wanted!"

"I don't think I could write a poem to save my life," Julie said. *No, darling girl, no time for a poem. Just me, saying I'm sorry* . . . The words echoed in her head, and a new thought suddenly struck her. Could *Uncle David* have put the message in the bottle and signed it *Jack* as a reference to the "jack-of-all-trades" that Aunt Nadine used to call him? Maybe the note was part of a game he'd made up years ago? Maybe he sealed the note into the perfume bottle and dropped it into the river for Aunt Nadine to find—but she never had?

Maybe Dolores didn't have anything to do with the bottle at all.

"Dolores," Julie said abruptly, tugging the red bottle out of her pocket. "Is this yours? I found it caught up in some roots in the riverbank. It sort of smells like your perfume."

"Oh, how pretty!" Dolores inspected the bottle. "I wish it were mine."

Julie studied the older girl. Was she telling the truth? She seemed to be genuinely intrigued. "This was inside it," Julie added, sliding the rolled message from her pocket and handing it to Dolores.

Dolores unrolled the scrap, her eyes widening as she read it.

"Do you think my Uncle David wrote it?" Julie asked.

"David?" Dolores sounded surprised. "It's signed 'Jack.'"

"I know, but you said David made up games and puzzles," Julie reminded her. "And Raymond told me he called people by different names . . ."

"But this isn't his handwriting."

"How do you know?" Julie asked.

"Because he let us read lots of the things he wrote. This handwriting looks more old-fashioned. No one does fancy script like that now." Dolores smoothed the scrap of paper with her fingers. "I wonder how long it was stuck in the riverbank.

And how it got there in the first place."

"And what does *'last hurrah'* mean, anyway?" Julie wondered.

"A last hurrah is like one last try, like a final act." Dolores paused, and then added, "I hope this was part of a game, because it sounds pretty desperate." She snapped her fingers. "I know—let's take this to Mariana and Leo Gage. They run the local history museum. I bet they can tell us how old it is."

Julie smiled. "Perfect!" It *was* perfect, too, because a trip to town would be a great way to keep Dolores out of the mine that morning so Raymond had more time to search. "But," she added, "let's not tell our parents about the bottle until we know more about it." If the message *did* lead somehow to gold, Julie wanted Raymond to be the one to share the happy news.

"Got it," said Dolores.

Dolores ran to the kitchen to announce she was taking Julie to Sonora.

Raymond walked in carrying a basket of eggs. Dolores smiled at him. "Want to come with us to Sonora?"

He met Julie's eyes and shook his head. "Nope. The henhouse needs a new latch."

Aunt Nadine turned from the sink in surprise. "It's not like you to miss a chance to stop in and see Pa."

Raymond shrugged. "And I need to make some repairs to the . . . um . . . tree house."

Mrs. Albright wiped the long table with a sponge. "Will you be okay walking back on your own, Julie? Because I know Dolores has to go to work. I don't want you getting lost!"

"I'll be fine," said Julie. "It's just one road. There's no way to get lost."

"Well, go get a dollar out of my handbag at the cottage," her mother said. "You girls can buy yourselves some ice cream."

Julie hugged her mom. "Thanks!"

Aunt Nadine cocked one eyebrow at Raymond. "Last chance to change your mind," she said. "Ice cream? Hello?"

Raymond smiled, but shook his head. "No thanks. Dolores will bring me one of those 'out of this world' brownies from the Galaxy. Won't you, Dolores?"

Dolores gave him a thumbs-up. "I always do," she said, grinning. "Since you do my chores when I'm working."

Raymond turned to leave the Big House, winking at Julie as he passed. "See you later . . . crocodiles."

"After a while, alligator," Julie tossed back. She watched him leave, and sent him silent wishes for good luck in the mine.

chapter 9

The Mother Lode

THE GIRLS WALKED side by side down the long rutted drive and onto the road that led to town. Dolores, normally chatty, was silent. "What's wrong?" Julie asked finally.

"I'm not sure," Dolores said slowly. "I get the feeling Raymond is up to something—and I'd love to know what. It's not like him to skip a trip into town!"

Julie felt her cheeks flush. She wanted to tell Dolores what Raymond was up to but didn't think she should. She said nothing and picked up her pace.

After walking about ten more minutes, they passed the cafe at the edge of the main street and strolled past antique shops and restaurants. Dolores told Julie how the old town had been settled by gold miners who had come from Sonora, Mexico, back in 1848. "Thousands more came from the east coast. My great-great-grandfather was one of the settlers. It's one reason I like the museum so much," she said. "It's my history in there, too."

At the museum, Dolores introduced Julie to Mariana and Leo Gage, the gray-haired couple who ran it. "Well, hello, Dolores! Haven't seen you in a while. How are things at the ranch?"

"Okay," Dolores replied. "I'm working part-time at the Galaxy now. This is my friend Julie. She's visiting from San Francisco."

"Welcome to the Mother Lode Museum!" Leo Gage smiled at Julie. "Come on in and look around."

Julie was already studying the displays with fascination. A sign explained that the Mother Lode Saloon had been where gold miners came to drink and eat more than a century ago. It was still set up now as if tired men would come bursting through the swinging doors any minute. Wooden shelves held empty glass bottles, and the potbellied stove in the corner had a tin coffeepot on top. Battered wooden tables with stools stood in the middle of the room as if miners might sit there to catch up with friends. Glass-topped cabinets held old clothing, shoes, and gold-mining tools. "It's like a time portal!" exclaimed Julie.

"That's the best compliment," said Mariana. "We want you to feel you could just slip back into history here."

"It looks like it could still be a restaurant," Julie marveled. "Tourists would love eating here."

"Well, they did, until Eli Coker opened his cafe two years ago and nearly put us out of business. Now we mostly serve coffee and lemonade to old-timers like us." Mariana laughed ruefully. "That cafe with its glitzy space-age stuff makes the big money."

Dolores stole a swift glance at her watch. "Speaking of which, I need to get there soon for my shift. Julie, show them your bottle. Maybe they can tell how old it is."

Julie dug in her pocket for the bottle and little scroll of paper. She unrolled the note and read it aloud to the Gages. "What do you think it means?" she asked.

Leo took the bottle and note in his hands and studied them for what seemed like a very long time. "My goodness, this is a find indeed," he said finally. He looked up at Julie. "I'd say you've struck the mother lode."

Julie's heart leaped. *Raymond should be here!* she thought. "You mean it leads to gold?"

"No, no, nothing like that." Leo shook his head. "I just meant that if you want to *sell* these to me, I'll pay a nice price. How about ten smackeroos?"

Julie blinked. Ten dollars wasn't exactly a fortune, but it was more than she was used to having at one time. "Why do you want them?" she asked.

"They're local history. I'd put them straight into the museum display. Tourists love anything about the old gold miners."

"But I found the bottle in the river," Julie said. "How can you be sure it's that old?"

Leo Gage turned the bottle upside down. "See this little bump on the bottom?" he said. "It's the mark left by the pipe the glassmaker blew through as he made the bottle. Modern bottles are manufactured a different way, so when I see this bump, I know a bottle is from Gold Rush times or earlier." He let the girls run their fingers over the bottom of the red glass to feel the little bump.

"And the message inside?" asked Julie. "The paper doesn't look that old."

Leo smoothed the note with his broad palm. "This paper is well-preserved because the wax kept out the air. It's hardly yellowed with age at all."

"That's what made me think it could have been

written by someone recently," Julie said.

Mariana peered at the note's loopy script. "No, the handwriting is definitely nineteenth century. That's how people were taught to write back then. In fact, I'm wondering if this note might be connected to the tragedy of 1852."

"The mine collapse, you mean?" asked Dolores.

"Yes," said Leo. He turned to Julie. "The locals know the story, but you'll be interested, since you're staying at Gold Moon Ranch. It happened the winter of 1852, when some men from Sonora decided to extend the mine. While they were in the mountain, drilling and blasting, a rainstorm came up and the river flooded. The supports holding up the mine shaft collapsed, and the men were trapped inside. No one ever knew for sure who all was in there."

"I've heard about that," Julie told him. "Wasn't there any way out?"

Leo shrugged. "These mountains are honeycombed with mine shafts and tunnels, but they might have been hard to reach in the rising water. It's not known if anyone survived that flood. Mariana's right; this note could have been written by one of those fellas." He held up the red bottle to the light. "A miner might have bought perfume from a traveling peddler, planning to give it to his sweetheart when he came home."

Julie nodded slowly. She realized now that the letter most likely was not part of a game or a story, and she felt a stab of sadness imagining what must have happened to the man who wrote it. The "last hurrah" might have been his decision to have one more try in the mine, hoping that this would be the big break, the time he'd find a fortune. He'd had a bottle of perfume for his wife in his pack when the rain-swollen river flooded the mine. He dumped out the perfume, wrote the note, and used the wax from his candle to seal the note inside the bottle. "But how did the bottle end up in the riverbank?" she wondered aloud.

"Probably the floodwater washed it out of the mine," Dolores said.

"So how about it, young lady?" Leo asked Julie. "Ten bucks for that piece of history?"

The money would help pay the ranch's taxes, Julie thought. And she *had* found the bottle on the ranch, so it would be right to give the money to the ranchers. But she didn't think she should sell it without first checking with Raymond. "Thanks, I'll think it over," she told Leo.

"Oh, my gosh," Dolores exclaimed, standing up. "I'd better run, or Mr. Coker's going to be waiting at the door of the cafe, tapping his foot and frowning at his silly rocket watch."

The girls said good-bye and left the Mother Lode. The sun was high in the sky, and the day had turned hot. "Whew!" said Julie, lifting her heavy blond ponytail off her neck. She looked enviously at Dolores's puff of dark hair that left her graceful neck bare.

A battered white pickup truck pulled up alongside them and tooted its horn. Lettering on its side said, "Fox Construction." "Hey there," said the driver. He was middle-aged, with a sunburned nose. His graying hair was pulled back in a ponytail. "Need a lift? I'm headed past the ranch."

Dolores walked to the truck's open window with a smile.

"Come meet Chris!" she called to Julie. "He lived at the ranch for years, and we miss him like anything. This is Julie," she told the man in the pickup. "Raymond's cousin. She could use a ride."

He nodded at Julie. "Hey there. I'd shake your hand but as you can see, I'm out of commission." He held up his right hand, which was swathed in a thick bandage. "Someone's always getting hurt doing construction. But a guy's gotta do what a guy's gotta do to earn a living, right?"

"We're trying to make a living, too," said Dolores. "Money's tight, so I'm working at the cafe, and now we're opening a shop. Julie's mom is helping get it started."

"Still the same, then?" Chris said. "Everybody working their tails off, but no money coming in? I have to admit, I dig making real bucks since I left Gold Moon. My brother Denny and me, we've got contracts for big housing developments going up on these mountainsides. A few more good jobs and we'll be living on easy street."

"We wish you'd move back, Chris," sighed Dolores.

Chris hooted. "Been there, done that! The ranch was fun while it lasted, I'll give you that. But it's really time you all sold that place. You've had some good offers, I hear. The land would make a great resort."

"A resort! No way would we let that happen," Dolores said. "Anyway, my shift's starting. I've got to go in—oh, Julie, hang on a minute. Will you take Raymond his brownie?"

Dolores ran inside and was back a moment later with three large brownies wrapped in napkins. "There's one for you too, Chris. See you later, Julie."

"Hop in," Chris said, leaning over to open the door. As Julie climbed into the front seat beside him, the thought crossed her mind that she would never do this in San Francisco—get into a truck like this with someone she didn't know—but since Dolores knew and liked Chris, Julie felt safe. How nice it must be to grow up in a place like this, where everyone knew each other!

"So you and your mom are thinking of joining the ranch?" Chris asked after they'd driven a few minutes in silence. "Giving up the evils of civilization?" His jaw tensed when he had to shift gears with his bandaged hand, but he steered easily up the winding road.

"No, we're just helping out," Julie told him.

The truck spun around a curve, and then shot up the long drive to the commune, spraying gravel.

"Here we are," said Chris. "Home sweet home."

Julie climbed down from the cab, carrying the brownies Dolores had wrapped for her and Raymond. "Thanks for the ride," she said.

"You're very welcome." Chris jumped out and slammed the door. "I think I'll just stop in and say hello."

Before Julie and Chris reached the porch, Viking Vicky came striding around the side of the Big House, yelling at the top of her lungs: "This is the last straw!"

chapter 10
Vanished!

JULIE RACED TOWARD Vicky. "What's wrong?"

"It's Buttercup," Vicky shouted. "She's gone!" She strode into the Big House, tracking muddy footprints across the kitchen floor, and collapsed into a chair. "Mamie's alone in her pen. Buttercup isn't there!"

"Was the gate accidentally left open?" asked Rose, coming forward to slip a towel under Vicky's muddy boots.

"The gate was closed and latched," Vicky said glumly. She pulled off her boots and stood them on the towel.

"So it was deliberate," said Allen, his voice tight. Then he noticed the former rancher standing behind Julie. "Hey, Chris! Good to see you, man."

"Looks like I've come at a bad time," Chris said.

"These days, seems like it's one bad time after another." Aunt Nadine's voice was weary. "You're lucky you left when you did."

"But who would steal a calf?" Julie asked.

Vicky tossed a scrap of paper onto the table. "This might tell us. I found it inside the barn."

They all looked at another torn piece of napkin from the Galaxy Cafe.

"This is too much," said Rose, putting her hands on her hips. "It's as if Eli Coker *wants* us to know it's him." She turned to her husband. "Allen, we need to alert the police. This is one of those times when I wish we had a phone up here."

"I can report it for you when I drive back into town," said Chris.

"I'll walk you to your truck," said Vicky, slipping on a pair of sandals from the pile by the door. The ranchers thanked Chris and said good-bye. He and

Vicky left the Big House and headed back to the parking area.

"I don't get it," Aunt Nadine said. "We've been here all day. You'd think somebody would've noticed Eli Coker—or any intruder—driving up here. But the dogs didn't bark."

Julie felt a now-familiar unease. *Not a single dog barked? But that must mean*—she shook her head, pushing away the unwelcome thought.

"I wonder how long the calf has been missing," Mrs. Albright said. "When did anyone last see her?"

"Raymond always feeds the animals early in the morning," Aunt Nadine replied. "The calf must have been there then, or he would have said something."

"Where is Raymond, anyway?" asked Julie, looking around the room.

"Here!" Raymond called, running into the kitchen from the back of the house. His cheeks were flushed.

Julie raised her brows in a silent question. *Did you find gold?*

He gave her a thumbs-up but waggled it uncertainly.

He's found something, Julie thought, handing him one of the napkin-wrapped brownies. "This is from Dolores," she said, unwrapping the other brownie to eat herself. She stuffed the napkin into her pocket.

"Dolores is my hero!" Raymond said, taking a big bite. Then he looked around the room at all the others. "What's going on?"

"Buttercup is gone," Aunt Nadine said, and filled him in on what had happened.

But Raymond seemed oddly unconcerned. He stuffed the rest of the brownie into his mouth, then crumpled his napkin and shot it like a basketball toward the trash can in the corner. Then he simply walked back outside.

Chris's truck spit gravel as it left the parking

area, and Viking Vicky came back into the Big House. She smiled at them as she stooped to pick up Raymond's crumpled napkin. "Who's the litterbug?" she asked, smoothing out the creases and laying the napkin on the table.

Julie walked out onto the porch, hoping to find Raymond there, but he was already partway down the path toward the cottages. "Let's go search for Buttercup," she called, hurrying to catch up.

Raymond hesitated. His eyes had a gleam to them. "Why don't you get started? Search the woods. I'll find you later."

"I don't even know where to start," Julie said. "Besides, something's giving me the creeps."

"What?" Raymond sounded impatient.

"Vicky thinks Mr. Coker must have come here and stolen Buttercup, because she found that scrap of napkin in the barn. But your mom said the dogs didn't bark. Not one!"

"So?" said Raymond.

Julie felt a shiver along her shoulder blades. "That means whoever took Buttercup was someone the dogs knew." Raymond stared at her blankly for a moment, then turned and darted off without answering. "Hey, aren't you going to help me?" she called after him.

"I've got something to do," he yelled back.

Julie stared after him, perplexed. Raymond *loved* Buttercup. Why did he seem so unconcerned at the news that she was missing? He'd just gobbled his brownie and tossed his crumpled napkin . . .

Another unwelcome thought poked at Julie, impossible to push away. She reached into her pocket and removed the napkin she'd shoved there. Mr. Coker and Dolores weren't the only ones who had access to Galaxy napkins. *Raymond did, too.* Had Raymond taken Buttercup? And if so, why?

Instantly, a reason occurred to her. Raymond said his father had a special way with animals. Maybe he thought if the calf went missing, Aunt

Nadine might beg Uncle David to help in the search. Or if things got hard enough at the ranch, maybe he thought Nadine might agree to move to town, and his family would be together again.

Julie thought back to the other things that had happened—the escaped chickens, the empty beehives. Like the cut clotheslines, they all seemed like childish pranks. She felt dizzy as another thought struck her. Could Raymond have been behind *all* the acts of sabotage? Could they all be part of a plan to reunite his mother and father? Maybe Dolores had nothing to do with any of it.

Julie's heart felt suddenly heavy. Her cousin didn't seem like the kind of boy who would try to frame someone else for trouble he himself was causing. *But the thing is,* she realized, *I just don't know Raymond well enough to know what he might do.*

Julie set off alone and searched the vegetable gardens. She passed the empty beehives and the chicken coop. She even looked inside the playroom and the schoolroom, then stopped at the pen where Mamie stood bellowing for her calf. "Poor Mamie," murmured Julie, rubbing the cow's soft nose.

There was no sign of Buttercup anywhere. It was as if she'd vanished into thin air. And yet, of course, she hadn't.

Julie frowned at Mamie, alone in the stall. Someone had opened the door, but surely Buttercup wouldn't just wander off, would she? Every time Julie had seen the calf, she stayed close to her mother. That meant someone must have *led* Buttercup away. And since the calf had not come back to Mamie on her own, that meant she had to be penned up or tied up somewhere.

Julie stuck her hand in her pocket and rubbed the glass bottle as if it would bring her good luck. She hated to think of the little calf all alone somewhere. She would be missing Mamie! She would need milk, or at least water . . .

The river! Raymond loved the calf and would

want to keep her safe. Maybe that's where he'd leave an animal so it wouldn't be without water, Julie reasoned.

She left the barn and set off into the woods. The path was dry, but yesterday's rain had left muddy puddles near the riverbank. As Julie rounded the bend and came in sight of the river, a cry reached her ears.

Julie hurried down to the water's edge. "Buttercup?" she called. "Buttercup, is that you?"

Yes! There, tethered to a tree beside the river, was the calf. She raised her head and bleated mournfully when she saw Julie.

Julie rushed to untie her. "Oh, Buttercup, are you okay?" She stroked the calf's soft neck. Buttercup's large eyes were shadowed with distress. "Let's get you back to your mama," Julie said. She tugged on the rope and the calf eagerly followed her up the steep path to the main trail, as if she knew she was going home.

When she reached the barn, Julie called to Jet in the meadow. He came running and checked out the calf. "No injuries," he said with relief. "So where was she?"

"Tied up by the river," Julie told him.

Jet's lips tightened as he reunited Buttercup with Mamie and tossed them some hay. Then he led the way back to the Big House, calling, "Julie found Buttercup!"

As Julie stepped into the kitchen, Rose shook her head and pointed to Julie's sandals, muddy from the riverbank. "Take your shoes off, honey," Rose said. "Leave them on the porch."

Aunt Nadine put her arm around Julie's shoulders. "How did you find her?"

Everyone applauded after Julie told the story, but still her heart felt heavy. Her cousin was not clapping for her. He was not even in the room.

Where is Raymond? she wondered. *And what is he up to?*

chapter 11
Suspicions

LATER THAT EVENING, the ranchers gathered as usual in the meadow. Viking Vicky and Mrs. Albright sang a duet and Rose and Dolores joined in, harmonizing.

Julie lay back and hummed along. The moon hung low and looked, she thought, just like a big gold coin. But she couldn't relax. Raymond hadn't helped look for the calf, and he wasn't here with the others, singing in the meadow. Her suspicions weighed on her more heavily than before.

Mrs. Albright and Aunt Nadine said good night and headed to the bathhouse. Before joining them, Julie helped Rose carry blankets into the Big House. The notebook her mom and Vicky had used for planning the new shop was lying open on a kitchen table. Curious, she stopped to flip through the pages of lists the women had made. Seeing their tidy columns of writing, it struck Julie that it might help her to figure out what was going on at the ranch if she also made a list. She ripped out a blank sheet of paper and took it with her.

As she entered the cottage, she heard a loud banging sound. She climbed the ladder to the loft and found Raymond there, kneeling on the floor by his bed, a hammer in his hand. He was struggling to open a metal box.

"What on earth . . ." she began.

He jumped at the sound of her voice. "Rats! I wanted to have this box open by the time you got here. I've been working on it practically all day."

"What is it?"

"I found it stashed near the mine this morning, just past that flat rock near where you found the bottle! It was half hidden by ivy. I think it's *got* to be full of gold—it's heavy!"

A locked box! So that's what he'd been focused on instead of helping search for Buttercup. Julie knelt next to the box. The lid and latches were battered from Raymond's hammer, but Julie could make out a tiny symbol that had been stamped near the lock. It looked like the head of a dog, but the dents made it hard to tell what kind. "Maybe try pliers. You're just denting it with the hammer."

"I told you I'd find treasure!"

At the sound of laughter outside on the porch, Raymond jumped up and hid the hammer under his pillow. "They're back! I don't want them to see this until I get it open!"

"Julie? Raymond?" Aunt Nadine's voice called.

"We're here." Raymond tossed a sweatshirt over the box just before Aunt Nadine's head appeared at the top of the loft ladder.

"Just wanted you to know there's still hot water in the bath, if you'd like a wash," she said. "Julie, you get first dibs—since you're the hero of the day!"

"Oh, no thanks, I'm fine." Julie didn't really like the idea of bathing in water someone else had used, and she had become used to making do with warm water and soap on a washcloth at the sink.

"Why is she a hero?" Raymond asked.

"Didn't she tell you? She found Buttercup!" said Aunt Nadine.

"Cool!" said Raymond, but he didn't ask anything more. Julie narrowed her eyes. Was that because he already knew perfectly well where the calf had been hidden?

"All right, kids, sleep well," said Aunt Nadine.

Her head vanished, and then Mrs. Albright called, "Good-night up there!"

"'Night, Mom," Julie called back.

Raymond pulled the sweatshirt off the metal box and sat there, studying the latch. "My pa could get this open," he whispered in frustration. "He can pick any lock! And if there's enough gold in here, then Pa won't need to work in town and can come back here . . ." His voice trailed off. "I'd give anything for that to happen."

"Anything?" whispered Julie softly. She didn't want to, but she knew she needed to ask Raymond about Buttercup, and everything else that had happened at the ranch. If he was responsible, then she needed to try to put a stop to it before something really bad happened—to the ranch or to her cousin himself.

She swallowed hard. "Raymond, I hate to have to ask this, but did you take Buttercup?"

Raymond turned away from the metal box and faced her. "Why on earth would I do that?"

"Well, so maybe your mom will see how much your dad is needed here and beg him to come back. Or maybe if there's too much trouble, she'll want to leave the ranch and move to town with him," Julie speculated.

Raymond snorted. "Some cousin you are. Some friend!" His cheeks were flushed.

With guilt? Julie wondered. "I'm only asking because I care about you," she said gently. "You didn't help look for Buttercup."

He glared at her. "I wanted to get the box open without anyone seeing. I'm trying to *solve* problems around here—not *make* them! And I'd never put any of our animals at risk. If you think I would, then you don't know me at all."

"Well, that's the trouble," Julie murmured. "I don't really know you. But I want to!"

He shook his head. "I thought I could trust you. I thought you wanted to help!"

"I do want to help! In fact, the museum owners offered me ten dollars for the bottle, and I was thinking I could give it to you to help pay the taxes!"

"Keep your bottle *and* your money," Raymond hissed, shoving the box under his bed. "I'll figure things out for myself!" He climbed into his bed, blew out the lamp, and turned his back to her.

Julie could feel his anger like a wall between them. But was he offended because he was innocent of her accusations? Or was he angry because she'd discovered his secret? Warring feelings swirled in her chest. Without even visiting the bathhouse to brush her teeth or change into her pajamas, she settled herself in her cot and propped her flashlight to shine on the paper she'd brought from the Big House. Using her book as a writing surface, Julie started a list of everything that was bothering her.

The paper napkins: Was Mr. Coker sneaking onto the property, causing trouble so the ranchers would give up and sell their land to him? Why would he leave napkins behind? That just seemed so careless. *It's almost as if he* wants *people to think it's him,* Julie thought. *Or someone else wants them to.*

The dogs had not barked: If Mr. Coker wasn't behind the sabotage, then one of the ranchers must be causing the trouble. Any of them had the opportunity—but only Raymond and Dolores seemed to have any reason to do it. Raymond wanted his parents back together. He might think the troubles would do the trick. Dolores might want to get back at Mr. Coker.

The mine: Was someone besides Raymond looking for gold? Was it Dolores? Julie still couldn't rule that out. Whoever it was, how had he or she gotten behind the collapsed wall?

The letter and the bottle: The Gages thought the bottle belonged to a miner over one hundred years ago. But was it somehow connected to what was going on in the mine *now*?

Other things niggled at her, bits of information that didn't seem to fit anywhere. *The blood on the handkerchief near the mine. The locked metal box. And what, if anything, does the sabotage have to do with what's happening at the mine?*

She must have dozed, because the creak of the ladder woke her. The door downstairs closed with a soft click. She looked over at her cousin's empty bed and sighed. Maybe he was going back to the mine. Or maybe he was just heading to the barn—that was where he went when he was upset. Either way, Julie knew Raymond would not want her company tonight. She had been just getting to know her cousin, and now she had ruined everything between them.

chapter 12
Where Is Raymond?

IN THE MORNING, Raymond's bed was empty. Julie got dressed and went out on the porch where her mom and Aunt Nadine sat chatting.

"Where's Raymond?" Julie asked.

"He's probably already at the Big House eating breakfast," Aunt Nadine said. "Let's go get some before it's all gone!"

The sky was overcast, and the air felt heavy as they walked. "Looks like rain again today," Aunt Nadine said with surprise. "So unusual for summer, but great for the garden."

In the Big House, Jet and Bonnie were flipping pancakes, and Julie accepted a stack with thanks. Dolores was finishing off her own stack, studded with blackberries.

"Raymond under the weather?" Allen asked, frowning. "He didn't get the eggs this morning, so I had to do it."

"And I had to feed the cows," Jet added.

"That's strange," said Aunt Nadine. "I wonder where he is?"

Julie paused in mid bite. If Raymond had slept in the barn as he often did, the ranchers would surely have seen him. Could he still be in the mine?

Dolores drained her cup of tea and stood up. "I've got to hurry. Breakfast shift."

"Take a poncho," said Rose. "Look how dark the sky's getting."

"I'll look for Raymond," said Julie.

"Thanks, dear," said Aunt Nadine. "It's not like him to ditch his chores."

Julie hurried off down the path. What could Raymond have been doing in the mine all night? Her heart thumped with worry. What if he'd met up with someone else in that dark tunnel? It wouldn't be Dolores, because she was in the Big House eating breakfast.

Julie reached the cave and ducked inside. The cool, damp dark closed around her as she moved to the entrance to the mine. She stopped in relief when she saw the barricade of boards. They were all in place. Raymond could not have gone into the mine and boarded the entrance back up, so that meant he was not here. But where was he?

Julie left the cave and crossed the swinging rope bridges to the tree house. "Raymond?" Carefully, she climbed the ladder to the tower, but he wasn't there either.

A misty drizzle had begun to fall, and the wind picked up. Shivering, Julie ran along the path by the river. She stood on the ridge and looked down at the clearing where she'd found the calf tied up. Dark water surged over the flat rock she'd stood on when she'd found the bottle stuck in the roots of the tree. The river raced past, and trees bent in the gusts of wind.

There, near the river, it struck Julie that she'd found the bottle because she was thinking like a miner, looking for gold. And she'd found Buttercup by thinking like Raymond. Maybe she could find Raymond by trying to think like him now. There were any number of places on the ranch where an angry kid could hide out, but . . . what if he wasn't hiding out at all? He'd said Uncle David would be able to pick the lock and get that metal box open! The box was heavy, but he'd carried it up from the mine, so he could have carried the box into town to his father's house. If so, he would have arrived at his dad's apartment late at night. The ranch had no phone, so Uncle David would not have been able to call the ranch to say Raymond was there. And Uncle David didn't have a car, so he couldn't bring Raymond home.

Thinking through the scenario, Julie smiled. Maybe right now Raymond and his father were having breakfast together, little piles of gold stacked on the table next to them, and soon Raymond would come walking home, triumphant, to pay the tax bill! She sorely hoped she was right.

On the way back to the Big House, Julie stopped at the cottage and climbed up into the loft to check under Raymond's bed. Sure enough, the metal box was gone. Thunder rumbled through the mountains, and she ran the rest of the way to the Big House.

"No luck?" Aunt Nadine asked in alarm when she saw Julie alone.

Julie shook her head. "No," she said. "But I think I know where he is. I bet he's gone to his dad's."

"It's not like him to run off like this," said Aunt Nadine. "But with all the trouble lately, Raymond really has been missing his pa. He needs David."

"He needs you both!" said Julie, her heart rising.

"Then let's go get him," Aunt Nadine said. "I don't want him walking home in this storm. It's about time you met your uncle, anyway."

Julie nodded, and took the umbrella her aunt handed her. As they dashed to the car, the wind blew rain beneath the umbrella, drenching them.

The windshield wipers made barely a dent against the downpour. Soon they passed the flashing neon sign of the Galaxy Cafe. Julie hoped Dolores had made it safely to work before the rain started. Aunt Nadine continued on to an apartment building on the far edge of town. Julie could see through the rain that it was bland and shabby, not quaint and historic.

Aunt Nadine's mood had shifted from worry to annoyance. "That boy's going to hear a piece of my mind," she said as she parked. "Staying out all night!"

Aunt Nadine will probably forget to scold Raymond when she sees all the gold, Julie thought to herself as she followed her aunt to Apartment 1B. Aunt Nadine reached out to knock, and the door swung open in a gust of wind that blew them both inside.

A gaunt man, sitting in a wheelchair with a book on his lap, looked startled. He rolled the chair to the door. "Well, good morning, Deenie," he said wryly. "I'd say 'do come in,' but I see you're already in." He smiled at Julie. "You must be my niece. Raymond told me you might be coming to the ranch!"

"Hello," Julie said. "Nice to meet you!" Her uncle was dark-haired like Raymond, with a bushy beard and friendly brown eyes.

"Sorry for barging in," Aunt Nadine said. She pushed the door closed. Their sodden shoes left puddles of water on Uncle David's floor, and Julie felt a peculiar nudge at the back of her mind. What was she trying to remember about water? About shoes? Something she'd seen? Something she'd heard?

"I've come for Raymond," Aunt Nadine said. "He left in the night without telling me where he was going! We've been quite worried."

Julie looked around the tidy studio apartment, expecting her cousin to appear, but there seemed to be nowhere to appear from. A kitchenette took up one corner, and a bookcase and guitar occupied another. A couch took up most of one wall, and the single bed under the window was covered with a tie-dyed spread. Through an open door Julie could see a small bathroom.

Clearly Raymond wasn't at his father's, unless he was hiding under the bed. There was no metal box on the table, and no pile of gold. Suddenly Julie felt queasy.

Aunt Nadine glanced uncertainly around the room. "If he isn't here, where is he? Julie said he left the cottage last night. She thought he'd come here—" Her voice cracked. "David, our boy is missing!"

Uncle David slowly stood up from his chair, bracing himself by holding on to the table, and walked over to her. "Come on, now," he said. "We'll find him. He can't have gone far."

Swiping away her tears, Aunt Nadine looked up at him in wonderment. *"You can walk?"*

"Barely. The physical therapy is slow, and I won't be running any races, but the doctors tell me my situation isn't hopeless. I'm working hard—for you and Raymond. I miss you."

Aunt Nadine searched his face as if seeing him for the first time. "I miss you, too."

Julie looked away from this unexpected tender moment. How she wished Raymond were here to see it!

The door banged open again on another gust of wind. Uncle David shut the door tightly before settling himself back in his wheelchair. "You've looked in the barn, and the tree house, of course?" he asked.

"Yes," Julie said.

"When did you see him last?"

Julie shifted her weight uncomfortably. "It was

late. He left after everyone else had gone to bed."

"He didn't tell you where he was going? Or why?" Uncle David's expression had grown more clouded, and Julie felt uncomfortable under his gaze. She'd vowed to keep Raymond's secret about the mine and the metal box. But that was when it was a happy secret. It didn't feel that way anymore. Raymond's parents were worried, and they needed to know the whole truth.

Julie began telling them everything—about the lights she and Raymond had seen near the mine, about his belief that there was still gold to be found, and about the mysterious, heavy box he'd hoped to surprise them with. She decided not to say anything about suspecting Raymond of the pranks at the ranch. That could stay between her and Raymond. For now, anyway.

"We had sort of a fight last night," Julie finished. "He was mad, and I thought he'd gone back to the mine without me."

Uncle David and Aunt Nadine looked at Julie openmouthed. "The mine?" Aunt Nadine's eyes were wide. "You two went *into the mine*?"

"Impossible!" barked Uncle David. "I boarded it up myself years ago. Nailed it up tight."

Julie pressed on despite their shocked expressions. "Someone must have loosened the nails, then, because we discovered a way to lift the boards right off them," she explained. "Luckily, the boards were still in place this morning, so I knew Raymond couldn't be in the mine after all."

"Thank heaven," Aunt Nadine said.

But Uncle David's face had gone pale. "That boarded-up entrance isn't the only way in," he said. "There's a tunnel into the mine—it opens right by the river. If he found that and he's inside, whoever else was in there might have him now. Even if he's alone, it's not safe. The walls aren't any more stable than they were a hundred years ago." He struggled out of his chair. "Get my walker, Nadine. We need to search that mine!"

chapter 13
Trapped!

UNCLE DAVID LEANED heavily on Aunt Nadine as they walked through the downpour to the car. Julie followed miserably behind them, rain mixing with the tears on her face. Her thoughts swirled as they drove back to the ranch. She and Raymond were in trouble now for having gone in the mine, but much worse than that, Raymond could be in danger. In their desperation to find him, his parents were united at last—and he was not even here to see it.

They entered the Big House, drenched, as the ranchers were already fixing lunch. Everyone there jumped up to welcome them. *They're so happy to see David!* Julie realized their small community was like a family, and the recent departures of so many members felt like a tear in the fabric of the clan. Each person counted.

But with the rain pelting down and Raymond missing, there was no time for happy reunions. Uncle David got everyone's attention with a penetrating whistle and explained about the mine.

"Get flashlights," he told them all. "And lanterns. Hurry!"

"Oh dear," said Vicky. "I'm sure there's no need to go into that dangerous mine . . ."

"But Raymond might be there!" cried Julie.

"David should not be going anywhere in this rain, with that walker!" Vicky looked distressed. "You all stay and keep him company. I'll go."

But the others were already grabbing ponchos, umbrellas, and flashlights and filing out of the house across the meadow to the woods. Instead, Vicky stayed behind, her expression grim. As everyone else left the Big House, her knife on the cutting board beat a sharp, hard rhythm.

The rain poured down. The sound of the river was deafening. Julie saw that the water level had risen, flooding the banks. *Thank goodness Buttercup is safe in the barn,* she thought.

Uncle David panted with the exertion and pain of walking. Julie stepped up to the barrier inside the cave and demonstrated how to lift the boards. "We found it like this," she said.

Allen scowled. "Somebody has tampered with these boards," he muttered.

They climbed into the tunnel. Uncle David needed help, and Allen hoisted him and the walker over the boards. The cool air and earthy scent enveloped them as they moved down the passage. Uncle David stopped to look up at the overhead beams. "Wow," he said. "Who installed these?"

Julie played her flashlight along the ceiling and saw in astonishment that some of the old wooden beams overhead were now fresh and new. "That's so weird," she said slowly. "I'm sure these weren't here the last time we came in. I remember because Raymond and I talked about how old the wood was."

"Did you talk about how the mine was boarded up for a good reason?" Aunt Nadine asked sharply. "Did you discuss how we'd told you the mine is *dangerous*?"

"I'm sorry," Julie murmured.

"This is a fine, professional job, and it will make the mine a lot safer," Uncle David said, turning to Allen. "But why shore up the mine after all these years? What's your plan?"

"I know nothing about this!" Allen protested.

"Well," said Uncle David. "Obviously *someone* knows about this and has arranged for the work to be done. I'd like to know who—and why."

Someone came here in the night and made the mine safer to work in—so they can find the gold! Julie kept this thought to herself. Everyone halted at the bend in the passage, where the avalanche of rock and earth had fallen over a century ago, trapping the miners.

"We heard tapping behind this collapsed wall," Julie told the others, pointing her light. The memory still made her shiver—even with the grown-ups nearby. "It sounded like digging. It sounded like somebody was there."

She strained to hear in the darkness. The sound of the rain and wind was extinguished inside the mine, but from behind the wall of earth and stone the sound came: *tap, tap, tap, tap!*

"There it is!" she cried.

The tapping was steady, and rapid, as if miners' pickaxes were falling faster and faster, trying to outpace the storm.

"Hmm," said Uncle David. "Sounds too regular to be digging. Must be water dripping behind the collapsed portion."

Everyone shouted: "Raymond! Raymond!" The walls echoed.

From behind the collapse there came a faint cry. *"Help!"*

"Raymond?" yelled Julie. How could he be *behind* the avalanche?

Aunt Nadine clutched Uncle David's arm.

"Where are you?" shouted Uncle David.

"Paaaa!" howled Raymond. His voice was stronger now. "You're here!" He was crying with relief. "I'm trapped!"

"We're both here, son," called Aunt Nadine. "We're all here!" She grabbed one of the old mining pickaxes from the small side room and heaved it at the rubble. "Who's got you? Who is it?"

"Ma!" came Raymond's thin voice from behind the avalanche. "I'm alone. A beam fell on my ankle. I think it's broken!"

Julie felt a wave of relief to know that no trespasser was holding Raymond captive. But her relief was short-lived. She pointed her flashlight down at the floor of the cave and felt her heart catch in her throat. A trickle of water was seeping through the rubble toward them. Outside the mine, the river was rising. Would it fill the cavern just as it had over a hundred years ago?

"How did you get back there?" Julie shouted.

"Julie? I knew you wouldn't be too mad to come looking for me!" His tearful voice was tinged with laughter.

Don't laugh yet, she thought. "I'm not mad," she called. "I didn't find you sooner because I thought you weren't here. The barricade was up!"

"I figured there had to be another entrance, near where I found the metal box, and where you found the bottle. And I was right."

"Down by the river!" cried Julie. "That's just what your dad said!"

"The entrance is tiny, but the passage runs into the mine shaft and—" Raymond's voice broke off in a groan. "Can you get me out? The water is pouring in!"

"How high is it now?" his father asked.

"About a foot. I'm sitting in it!" Raymond sounded panicked.

"Keep your head up," called Uncle David. "Come on, everybody. We've got to get to that other entrance."

"Oh, my poor boy." Aunt Nadine turned away from the rubble. "Let's go!"

"Go to that flat rock, Julie!" called Raymond. "Look behind the ivy!"

"We're on our way!" called Allen, darting ahead. Aunt Nadine raced after him.

"I'm staying here to keep you company, son," Uncle David said. "Just hang on."

Raymond's voice caught on a sob. "Thanks, Pa."

The ranchers hurried back to the entrance. The roar of the rising river was deafening. Julie led the others out of the cave and into the rain, picking her way along the path to the riverbank where she had discovered the bottle stuck in the roots.

She thought this was the same place, but it looked different with the water so high. She held on tightly to the exposed roots and worked her way down the bank, finally coming to stand on the broad rock. Water lapped over her feet.

"Careful, Julie!" shrieked her mother. "You'll fall in!"

Jet and Allen held on to the tree and leaned over to grab Julie's poncho. They steadied her as she knelt on the rock and pushed hanging vines to the side, and—yes, there was a gap in the rock.

"Here it is!" she shouted over the rushing river.

It was almost a cave, just big enough for a grown man to crawl into, but a short way in, large rocks had tumbled, blocking most of the entrance. The small space left looked like the sort of hole in which a fox or bobcat might shelter.

"The collapse looks recent," said Allen. He reached out to touch the slippery mud and damp, crumbled earth. "This is bad. We've got to get him out before the whole passage caves in."

Aunt Nadine climbed down on the rock and struggled to fit through the opening, but it was too small. Julie took a deep breath. "I can fit," she said.

She stuck her head inside the crevice and shouted for Raymond. "Can you hear me?"

His reply was faint. *"Hurry!"*

Mrs. Albright's face was ashen. "No, Julie—it isn't safe!"

The river flowed over the bank and splashed into the entrance. "I have to, Mom." Julie crouched, and the water surged around her knees. She edged sideways between the fallen rocks.

"Take this!" Aunt Nadine stuck her arm between the rocks to hand Julie a flashlight.

Julie was glad to have it. The only other light came from the opening behind her. Water sloshed around her calves. Bending low, she crept along the narrow passage. "Raymond?" she called. "I'm coming!"

"I see your light!" Raymond shouted.

She played her beam on old boards lining the passage and thought about the men who had dug this tunnel. Ahead of her she heard a cry of pain.

And there he was, illuminated in her flashlight, sitting on the ground in the muddy water. A heavy ceiling beam stuck up from the water near his leg. "Julie!" he cried. "I've never been so glad to see anybody!"

"Julie, is that you?" Uncle David's voice came through the fallen rubble. "Where are the others?"

She explained that the opening had crumbled. "Raymond and I can fit," she said, "but first we have to get this beam off him." She grabbed the end of the beam with both hands and tried to move it, but it was too heavy.

Julie pushed down flutters of panic. It wouldn't help now to start screaming. She could get out, but she wouldn't leave without Raymond. There must be a way to save both of them.

The water was nearly to her knees now. Raymond sat in water up to his chest. Water rolled toward them from the river, and the beam pinning Raymond shifted. He screamed in pain.

"What's *happening*?" Uncle David's voice was frantic.

The shifting beam gave Julie an idea. "Hold on," she told Raymond. "Wait for the water to rise even higher, then we'll try to lift the beam."

"I've tried all night to lift it," he cried. "It's too heavy!"

"I know, but the water is rising now. The beam will start to float, and we can lift it together!"

They sat silently for a few minutes, watching the water level inch higher, and the opposite end of the beam begin to rise with it. "It's time," Julie said tensely. "One, two, three, *now*!"

Julie pulled on the beam with all her might, and it floated upward. With a shout of relief, Raymond kicked his foot free.

"I'm out!" he cried.

"Hallelujah!" called Uncle David.

"We still need to get out of the mine," said Julie. The water was now nearly waist high. She grabbed Raymond's arm and towed him along back through the passage, bent double. He sobbed with pain, but tried his best to walk. "Just relax and try to float," Julie instructed, her heart pounding.

When they reached the opening at last, the ranchers and her mom were there, waiting. They helped Raymond wriggle between the boulders, grabbing Julie, too, as she slipped through. She could see now that Raymond's foot was badly swollen.

Completely sodden and streaked in mud, Julie stood on the rock, shivering. The rain on her face had never felt so good.

chapter 14

Mendings

JET HOISTED RAYMOND carefully up to the path, where he was engulfed in hugs from Aunt Nadine. Allen reached for Julie's hands and pulled her up the mud-slick riverbank, too. Then he hurried to the main entrance to help Uncle David.

They all slogged back to the Big House, with David hobbling between Jet and Nadine, and Raymond riding piggyback on Allen. Raymond was safe. Julie hated to think how close a call he'd had.

When they came through the door, Viking Vicky ran for a pile of dry towels.

"What in the world has happened?" she asked.

"I was trapped in the mine," Raymond told her as Allen lowered him carefully to a kitchen chair. "Julie saved me!"

"Oh my!" said Vicky. "That deserves some hot chocolate."

"Shoes off, everybody," Rose cautioned. "We don't want all this mud tracked inside!"

Even as everyone praised Julie's bravery, and her mother stroked Julie's hair, the back of Julie's neck prickled. What was it about muddy shoes she was trying to remember? She turned from the door to find Vicky pouring mugs of cocoa and offering bread and cheese.

"We'll just take a sandwich with us," Uncle David said. "We'll need to get Raymond straight to the doctor."

"Julie, can you please run to the cottage to get some dry clothes for him?" Aunt Nadine asked, holding out an umbrella. "Change clothes yourself while you're there."

Julie dashed through the rain to the cottage. Because the laundry had not yet been finished, her only dry clothes were the ones she'd been wearing the day before. She changed quickly and hurried back through the rain, hugging Raymond's dry shirt and pants to her chest with one arm and holding the umbrella aloft with the other.

After Aunt Nadine helped Raymond change, Allen carried him to the car. Uncle David followed haltingly with his walker, and Mrs. Albright walked beside him, holding her umbrella over both their heads. Julie ran after them. "Can I come?"

"Of course," said Aunt Nadine.

Raymond smiled as Julie squeezed into the backseat with him, but his pale face looked exhausted. Rather than tire him further with talking, Julie gazed out the rain-streaked window in silence. As they neared the clinic, they passed a small building where a familiar truck was parked. "Fox Construction," the truck's side panel read. It was the truck Chris had been driving the day before. Julie turned in her seat and looked out the back window. On the truck's tailgate was the construction company's logo: the outline of a fox's head inside a circle. Memory stirred: Where had she seen that same symbol recently?

The metal box! The little animal on the box wasn't a dog, it was a fox. The box belonged to Fox Construction! A picture was beginning to take shape in Julie's mind, but she found it hard to bring into focus.

Julie leaned close to whisper in Raymond's ear. "Where's the metal box? I didn't see it under your bed, and it wasn't at your dad's apartment when we went to his place to look for you."

"You went to Pa's apartment?"

"Your mom and I thought you might be there."

"Ma went, too?" Raymond's eyes widened.

"She was frantic. They both were."

Raymond closed his eyes briefly. "It's in the bottom of my dresser," he whispered.

They arrived at the clinic, and Raymond bit his lip against the pain as Julie and Aunt Nadine helped him inside. While Aunt Nadine went into the examining room, Julie sat with Uncle David in the waiting area.

"Uncle David?" Julie struggled to put her thoughts into words. "Something . . . strange is going on."

"What do you mean?" her uncle asked.

"Well, do you know Chris?"

"Chris Fox? Sure, I know him."

"I mean—do you like him?"

Uncle David looked puzzled. "Chris is a good guy. Lived at Gold Moon Ranch for years, and left around the time I did."

"I guess he's got a construction business now," said Julie.

"Yes, with his brother, Denny." Uncle David looked curiously at Julie. "You think that's strange?"

"No, but I met him yesterday, and then just now I saw the fox painted on the back of his truck. The same fox is stamped on the box Raymond found in the bushes outside the mine. The box is heavy. Raymond thinks there's gold in it."

Uncle David looked at Julie for a long moment. Then he sighed and spoke. "I'm afraid Raymond's going to be very disappointed. There's surely nothing but tools inside that box. In fact, that box probably explains who's behind the new construction inside the passage. Chris and Denny would certainly be able to replace old beams. They're excellent builders."

Julie nodded. "When Raymond and I saw lights in the mine in the middle of the night, that must have been when Chris and Denny were doing the ceiling repairs. But why would they be sneaking around and keeping it a secret?"

Uncle David frowned. "You're right, that doesn't make much sense."

"It does if they're searching for gold," Julie pointed out.

"Julie," Uncle David began gently, "believe me,

there is nothing to find. I lived near the mine as a child, and I explored practically every part. I know there's no gold left in that mine, and Chris Fox knows it, too."

Julie thought hard about Chris. His hand had been bandaged when he gave her a ride home, she remembered. And there'd been a bloody handkerchief on the path to the mine. Suddenly, another part of the picture was coming into focus. Chris must have hurt his hand at the mine and left his toolbox there. The bloody handkerchief had not come from Dolores's injury. So Dolores hadn't been at the mine. And she probably hadn't cut the clothesline, either, Julie realized.

Have I been wrong about Raymond, too? she asked herself.

Just then, Raymond ambled awkwardly into the waiting room on crutches, his ankle in a cast. Uncle David gave his son two thumbs up.

"Hope you'll share your wheelchair, Pa!"

Raymond exclaimed, and Julie couldn't help laughing.

They drove to Uncle David's apartment, and Raymond lay on the couch with his leg elevated. While Uncle David washed up in the bathroom, Aunt Nadine busied herself tidying the kitchen.

Julie knelt on the floor next to Raymond and filled him in on everything she had learned about the box and who it belonged to.

Raymond frowned. "So it was Chris Fox's light we saw at night. He and his brother could have parked out on the road so no one heard their truck."

Julie glanced over to the little kitchen, where Aunt Nadine was now cleaning the sink. The door to the bathroom was closed, and she could hear her uncle humming in the shower.

"Your dad says there's no gold in that mine. Period. And that the metal box only has tools in it.

"Darn." Raymond's face fell.

"Sorry," said Julie. "But it's weird, isn't it? All the secrecy about making the mine safe? All the sabotage at the ranch? I'm pretty sure they're connected somehow. And . . ." she took a deep breath and looked Raymond in the eye. "I'm also pretty sure you didn't take Buttercup."

He raised his dark brows. "Just *pretty sure*?"

"I'm *sorry,*" she whispered. Feeling her face flush, she pulled a heavy book from under a table near the couch and began flipping through it to hide her discomfort. The volume was a scrapbook. Julie studied photos of Raymond as a dark-haired toddler with his parents, much younger then, laughing in the bed of a pickup truck. She flipped a page and found a flower crown, its flowers faded and pressed flat. *Uncle David must have made that for Aunt Nadine,* she thought.

She turned another page and studied what had been glued there: a sepia-toned photograph and a heart-shaped sheet of paper with handwriting on it. The photograph showed a young man in a suit and top hat and a woman in a long, dark dress with full sleeves. Beneath her lacy bonnet her eyes shone.

Julie caught her breath. She bent and peered more closely at the handwriting. The paper was spotted with age, but the neatly penned script was clear. She recognized that handwriting.

Wonderingly, she read the poem aloud softly:

> ***There was a good man loved a cipher***
> ***But even more longed for a wifer . . .***
> ***My dear Colleen Lou,***
> ***Won't you please say "I do"?***
> ***And together we'll have a fine lifer!***

The paper was signed, in looping script,

> *Yours eternally, J.*

"What *is* this?" Julie blurted out.

"I never really looked at it before," said Raymond. "Ma?" he called. "What's this?"

Aunt Nadine walked over. "Oh," she said. "That's a family heirloom, from Pa's side of the family. It was written by his great-great-grandfather, Joaquin Sandoval, asking his wife to marry him. It's been in Pa's family for generations."

Uncle David limped out of the bathroom dressed in dry clothes. He settled himself back into his wheelchair with a sigh of relief. Then he saw Julie gazing at the poem. "Are you interested in limericks?" he asked.

Julie sank back onto the couch next to Raymond. She felt dazed. "Your great-great-grandfather wrote it? The one who went off to San Francisco and never came back?"

Uncle David looked surprised. "So you know our family story?"

"I told her the part about how he made a

fortune and vanished." Aunt Nadine walked to the window and stared out at the rain.

"There's more to that story," Uncle David said. "Once upon a time, a young man named Joaquin came from Mexico in search of gold, and he met an Irish girl whose family ran a laundry service for the miners. They struck up a friendship, and he fell in love. He thought it would be romantic to propose to her in a poem. So Jack—that's what he called himself in California—put his limerick in a bottle sealed with wax, and floated it to Colleen across the washtub while she was working."

Julie felt a jolt. *Joaquin Sandoval was called Jack!*

Aunt Nadine smiled. "David told me that romantic family story when we first met. Later, he asked me to marry him the same way—by writing me a poem. It's in that scrapbook, too."

"And you wrote back, saying yes." Uncle David's eyes twinkled.

Aunt Nadine's cheeks were pink. "Yes, but I

also said something else, remember? Jack Sandoval might have been a charming poet, but what good was that if he cared for gold more than he cared for his family? I said, *I'll marry you, David Stratton, but don't you be like him. Don't you ever leave me.* You laughed and promised you would always put family first."

She paused, as if deciding whether to go on. "But you did leave us," she added softly.

"Deenie," Uncle David said. "Please, let's not go over it again. I had to go to Vietnam, to find my brother. And unlike faithless old Jack, *I* came home."

"But that's the thing," Julie burst in. Excitement made her voice tremble. "Jack *wasn't* faithless! I think he *meant* to come home. I think his very last thoughts were of his family."

"What do you mean?" asked Aunt Nadine.

Julie felt in the pocket of the dry shorts she'd changed into earlier. The poem was still there from when she'd worn them the day before. "This message I found has the very same handwriting! Whoever wrote it loved his wife and meant to come home to her." After explaining how she found the perfume bottle, Julie laid the message from the bottle on the table next to the scrapbook. "See?" She traced the message with her finger, comparing it to the limerick.

There once was a lad strong and bold
Who left home to find pots of gold—
No, darling girl, no time for a poem.
Just me, saying I'm sorry for my one last hurrah.
I meant to bring you perfume in this bottle,
but now it carries a message instead.
God only knows if you'll receive it.
You were right all along.
Love's already made me rich.
If I ever get out, I'm coming home.

Yours eternally, Jack

Aunt Nadine and Uncle David bent their heads together over the poem. "Well, would you look at that!" said Uncle David. "It *is* the same handwriting, curlicues and all."

Aunt Nadine was silent for a long moment. "My goodness," she said finally. "Julie, I think you've just laid to rest an old family scandal! Jack must have said he was setting off for San Francisco with his fortune, planning to build the mansion he'd promised Colleen—but in the end he decided to join his buddies in one last quick try for even *more* gold."

"One last hurrah," murmured Julie.

"Exactly. He must have died when the mine flooded, and Colleen never knew he hadn't gone to San Francisco. She thought he had abandoned her."

"It's a sad story," Julie said.

"Yes," Uncle David said. "But we misjudged Joaquin Sandoval all these years . . . and maybe there's another family situation we've misjudged.

He reached for Aunt Nadine's hand and looked at her searchingly. "Eh, Deenie?"

Aunt Nadine looked down at her hand clasped in his, then slowly placed her other hand on top. "Not everything's as it seems," she agreed with a smile.

Julie looked away. She couldn't help smiling, too, when she saw Raymond watching his parents with eyes wide and full of hope.

chapter 15
Gotcha!

ON THE WAY back to the ranch, Aunt Nadine, Uncle David, Raymond, and Julie stopped at the cafe to pick up Dolores. While Raymond filled her in on all the amazing things that had happened, Julie listened quietly. Aunt Nadine and Uncle David were smiling at each other, Raymond was safe, and they'd solved the mystery of the message in the bottle! Everything should feel right, she reflected, but things were still going wrong for the ranchers. *Who's responsible?* she wondered. *And why?*

When they arrived at the ranch, Mom greeted Julie at the door of the Big House with a hug.

Rose hugged Uncle David. "I'm glad you're here!" she said. "I've lit the fire. This rain makes it feel like fall already. Wipe your feet, everybody!"

Aunt Nadine slipped off her shoes. She shook out their wet umbrellas and left them in the kitchen sink, then went to settle Raymond on the couch and help make Uncle David cozy by the fire. Julie slid out of her sandals, then stopped, staring at the line of wet shoes.

Rose was always telling people to wipe their feet. She'd reminded Julie when she returned from the river after finding Buttercup. She'd slipped a towel under Vicky's muddy boots when Vicky announced the calf was missing.

Vicky's muddy boots . . .

Julie remembered that yesterday the paths were dry when she had searched for Buttercup; her own shoes became muddy only down by the river, where Buttercup waited at the water's edge. But Vicky's shoes were muddy when she came into the house to report the calf was gone. That meant Vicky must have been down by the river. So why hadn't Vicky seen Buttercup and brought her home? There was only one way it made sense: if *Vicky* was the one who'd taken the calf in the first place.

Julie's heart pounded hard. She darted a look over at Vicky now—Vicky, who'd been the first to blame Mr. Coker for the problems at the ranch. Could the person behind it all really be their helpful new manager, Vicky?

Julie remembered the way Vicky had smoothed out the napkin Raymond had carelessly tossed toward the trash. She could have saved other napkins and left one behind at each scene of sabotage—hoping to make the ranchers suspect Mr. Coker. It made more sense to Julie than thinking Mr. Coker had left the napkins behind himself.

But why would Vicky go to all that trouble? What could she possibly have to gain? Julie stared out through the rain at the windswept meadow and thought about all the people who wanted this land. The ranchers themselves, of course. And Mr. Coker. There was also, she remembered, a person who'd angered the ranchers with a proposal to build an amusement park on the land.

Everyone, other than the ranchers, seemed to think the land should be developed. Even Chris Fox, who'd been a rancher himself, had said the place would make a great resort.

Recalling his words, Julie suddenly felt something click inside her. She reached out and picked up her mom's notebook, the one she'd written lists in with Vicky, which was still there on the kitchen table. Then she walked slowly down the hallway. She met Dolores just as she was returning from changing out of her work clothes.

Julie looked over her shoulder toward the kitchen to make sure they were out of earshot. "I think I've figured something out. Come with me to the library. I need to look at those books you found—the ones from the barn."

They were books no one admitted to owning. Books about hotel management and how to start a resort. *An amusement park is sort of like a resort,* Julie thought.

Dolores cocked her head and grinned. "So, maybe I didn't miss out on all the excitement after all?"

"Maybe not," said Julie. Together they hurried into the library.

Julie found the book titled *Resort Management* and opened it. The name on the flyleaf, written in a flowing hand, read: *A. V. King*. She leafed through her mother's notebook until she found the page of lists her mother and Vicky had made. The handwriting matched a list Vicky had written in the notebook.

Gotcha! thought Julie.

"What is it?" asked Dolores.

"Come with me," Julie whispered. "We've got almost all the proof we need."

"Proof of what?" Dolores whispered back.

Julie didn't answer. She stepped into the big

living room, where Raymond lay on the couch with the dogs on the floor next to him.

Aunt Nadine came in from the porch with the metal box from Raymond's dresser in her arms. She handed it to Uncle David, who sat in the battered armchair next to the couch.

"Seeing is believing," Uncle David told his son as he deftly picked the lock with a bent paper clip. Inside the box was a set of tools, just as he had predicted.

Raymond shrugged, and grinned at his dad.

Aunt Nadine settled herself next to Julie's mom on the big cushions by the fireplace. Julie knelt beside her. Casting a wary glance toward the kitchen, where the other ranchers were preparing dinner, she spoke in a low voice. "Someone wanted to build a theme park here, right?"

"That's right," said Aunt Nadine.

"Hey, I didn't hear about this," said Uncle David.

"Shh!" Julie nodded at the kitchen area, where the other ranchers were busy cooking. "Do you remember the person's name?" she whispered.

"No," said Aunt Nadine, "but Allen will." She sat up as if to call to him.

Julie put her hand on Aunt Nadine's arm. "Wait." She motioned for Dolores to come over and spoke to her softly. Dolores walked to the kitchen and spoke quietly to her father and mother.

Allen and Rose left the kitchen and came into the big room. "What's up?"

"Who wrote us about that gold-mining theme park?" Aunt Nadine asked. "Julie wants to know."

"Somebody called King," Allen said. "The letter's around here somewhere. I don't think there was a first name, just initials. Why?"

"Was it A. V. King?" Julie spoke the name softly.

"That's it," said Rose.

"Why are we whispering?" Raymond hissed from the couch.

Julie shot a glance toward the kitchen where Bonnie was now setting the table and baby Rainbow was banging spoons on a pot. Vicky and Jet were leaving the Big House to tend to the animals.

"I think I know who's behind the sabotage." Julie kept her voice low, but she felt better when the screen door closed behind Vicky. "I'm just not quite sure how to prove it." She told them about the mud.

Raymond's brow furrowed. "But Vicky's so nice."

"I don't think she's so nice," said Julie. "I think she took Buttercup. I think she's done everything else, too." Julie took a deep breath. "And—I don't think Vicky is really Vicky Prince at all!"

"What in the world do you mean?" asked Aunt Nadine.

"I found some books in the barn after Vicky arrived at the ranch," Dolores said. "Nobody seemed to know whose they were. They all have either Alma V. King or A. V. King written inside.

And A. V. King is the name of the person who wanted to buy this place and build a gold-mining theme park!"

Julie smiled grimly. "I'll bet you anything the *V* stands for Vicky." She showed them how the handwriting in the list matched the writing inside one of the books.

Julie's mom nodded. "You're one very observant girl."

"She's a genius!" Rose took Julie's face in her hands and planted a big kiss on each cheek.

"But what do we do now?" fretted Dolores. "How do we trap Vicky?"

"We need a plan," Julie said. "One as sneaky as she is."

"Leave it to me," said Uncle David. "I'll cook up a plan by dinnertime."

chapter 16

Banishment and New Beginnings

AT DINNER, EVERYONE dove into big bowls of spicy chili and salad and hot buttered cornbread. Julie sat between Dolores and Raymond, who'd insisted he felt well enough to come to the table. "I'm not missing the showdown!" he whispered to Julie.

Julie held several things on her lap: the scrapbook, the glass bottle, and the message.

Aunt Nadine raised her glass. "To Julie," she said, her voice trembling. "For her brave rescue of our boy. Thank you, dear heart!"

The ranchers applauded, and Julie flushed.

"And to Raymond," said Uncle David. "A speedy recovery!"

Rose proposed a toast to Uncle David, saying

how nice it was that he was back among them, even if only for dinner. All the ranchers clinked their glasses.

Then Julie took a deep breath and pinged her fork against her water glass. Conversation came to a stop. It was time to put Uncle David's plan into action.

"I want to tell you a story," she began, then faltered. She glanced at Raymond, who nodded. And suddenly she didn't feel nervous at all.

She held up the bottle that had been in her lap. Evening sunlight slanting through the kitchen windows made it gleam like a ruby in her hand. "I found this bottle stuck in the roots of a tree along the riverbank. And inside was . . . this." She held up the handwritten note. "Raymond hoped it was a treasure map leading to gold! It isn't, but it does have something to do with gold."

Everyone craned their necks to look at the objects in Julie's hand. After a moment, Julie set them down. She opened the scrapbook to the page with Joaquin Sandoval's poem and held it up so everyone could see. "This has been in my uncle's family for over a hundred years!"

"Yes," said Uncle David with a rueful smile. "My great-great-grandfather made a fortune in gold, then set off for San Francisco to build his wife a mansion. No one ever heard from him again. It was a family scandal."

"Not anymore!" Julie read the marriage proposal limerick aloud before passing the scrapbook around the table. "The exciting thing I learned today is that the message in the bottle was written by the same man who wrote this limerick. The handwriting matches exactly!"

Aunt Nadine explained. "We figure that Jack decided to try his luck in the mine just one more time before heading to San Francisco. This time his luck ran out. He was trapped in the mine and sent a desperate message of love to his wife. So now there's a new ending to our old family tale."

"A man who seemed a villain turns out to be a good guy after all," said Uncle David.

"An important lesson, isn't it?" Aunt Nadine looked around the table at each commune member. "Sometimes things just aren't what they seem."

Now Dolores nudged Julie under the table in a signal to keep going. Julie cleared her throat. "In the limerick we learn that Colleen's middle name was Lou," she said gaily. "I think it would be fun to go around the table and say what *our* middle names are! Mine is Anne. What about the rest of you?"

Raymond jumped right in: "Mine is Owen!"

Dolores spoke up brightly: "I'm Dolores Cassandra! Cassandra means 'prophetess.'"

"I'm Rosemary Octavia," Rose said. "What were my parents *thinking*?"

Bonnie revealed her real name was Bonita Catherine. Her husband, Jet, shared that he was Jedediah James.

Around the table they went. Nadine Marie. David John. The ranchers laughed as they discovered each other's middle names. Julie smiled gaily, but she felt tense inside.

Allen rolled his eyes when it was his turn. "Allen is my middle name. My first name is *Aloysius*, but I have never once used it!" He paused, then added, "I don't think I can even spell it!"

The ranchers roared with laughter.

Vicky was last. "I'm like you, Allen," Vicky said. "Victoria's my middle name. I use it because my mother and I have the same first name. It gets confusing."

"Too confusing to have two Almas," said Uncle David. "Right, Vicky? You and your mother are both Alma Victoria."

"Yes . . ." Vicky suddenly looked puzzled. "But how did you know?"

This was the moment Julie had been waiting for. "Such a pretty name. *Alma Victoria King*."

"Why, thank you," said Vicky—and with that she had fallen into their trap.

"But isn't she Vicky *Prince*?" objected Dolores, following the script they'd prepared.

Julie looked to Uncle David. He was one of the founding members of the commune, and he took the lead naturally, as if he'd never been away. "My friends, the person who has lived among you as Vicky Prince admits she is really Alma Victoria King—also known as A. V. King!"

"Hey!" Jet stood up from the table. "The theme park guy?"

Mrs. Albright spoke up. "A. V. King turns out not to be a guy at all," she announced, satisfaction in her voice. "Julie is the one who figured it out."

"What I figured out," said Julie, "is that a lot of things aren't what they seem. Vicky didn't come here to help. She came here to get you to sell the land—to her. *She's* the one who's been causing all the trouble."

Vicky's face was splotched with red. Her voice rang out loud and angry. "You have no proof of that!"

"The books that turned up in the barn after you came here all have A. V. King or Alma King written on the first page," Uncle David said calmly.

"In *your* handwriting!" Julie held up the spiral notebook, and Vicky shot her a dagger glance.

"A king never likes being demoted to a prince," said Uncle David. "But there's a lot more to the story, as Julie discovered. What I'm wondering is whether you came here on your own or whether the Fox brothers are your partners."

Vicky's laugh was hard and scornful. "You think I need Chris and Denny Fox to build a business? I hired them to make the mine safer. That's it. As you've seen today, it's very dangerous! You should thank me for having them make improvements."

"Raymond wouldn't have been lured down to

the mine if it hadn't been for you." Aunt Nadine's voice was indignant. "And you don't own this land. How *dare* you?"

"You'd sell to me eventually." Vicky sat back in her chair and stared around the table at them. "You'd see you're destined to fail."

Julie cleared her throat. "She tried to buy the land last year for her amusement park, but when no one would sell, she came to live here under a different name, acting helpful to earn your trust. But she was secretly causing trouble so you'd want to sell! When she learned Mr. Coker also wanted to buy the ranch, she started pinning the blame on him. She wanted to make sure you'd never sell to him."

The ranchers stared at Vicky incredulously. "Vicky, *really*?" asked Bonnie.

Vicky shrugged. "My offer is excellent, and I have a fine plan for this place. You people need to admit that you've failed. It's time to move on."

At the ranchers' protests, Vicky folded her arms

defiantly. "I don't see what you're all worked up about. I'd be doing you a favor by buying this land. I could make a really amazing theme park: tours into the mine, rafting rides on the river, roller coasters in the meadow, a restaurant in the Big House selling cotton candy, pizza, snow cones—"

Uncle David cut her off. "You should be arrested. You've trespassed on ranch property, misused funds to pay the Fox brothers to work in the mine—and misled people about your identity."

"Just pack up your stuff and get out of here," said Aunt Nadine. "Don't show your face here again, or I promise you we *will* call the police."

Banished, thought Julie with satisfaction. *Exactly what Vicky deserves.*

The rain had finally stopped, and everybody waited outside Vicky's cottage while she threw her things into suitcases. Then Jet drove Vicky down the mountain to the bus station. No one said good-bye.

Afterward, Julie sat with Dolores, Raymond, and his family in the living room, drinking hot chocolate. Julie felt the sweetness spread through her, and with it relief that her awful suspicions about her new friends had been unfounded. She studied the perfume bottle and note, still on the table, and decided there was just one more thing she needed to do.

"I'd like you to keep these," she said, handing the bottle and note to Uncle David. "You can put the note in the scrapbook along with the marriage proposal and wedding photograph."

"Thank you," Uncle David said solemnly. "We'll keep the scrapbook right here in our cottage, and you can look at it any time you visit."

"In *our* cottage?" Raymond repeated, his eyes wide and full of hope.

Uncle David reached over and mussed

Raymond's shaggy hair. "Your mother and I think it's high time I move back here, son," he said. "*Somebody's* got to give you a haircut."

"Your pa is going to keep working in town," Aunt Nadine told Raymond. "But he'll come home at night to us."

Julie could only imagine how Raymond must feel. Her own heart felt as if it were ready to burst with happiness.

The week that followed seemed tame after everything that had happened. Yet Julie was anything but bored. She finally learned to milk a cow; she helped card and spin wool into balls of soft yarn; she woke early to gather eggs for breakfast. Dolores took her rafting on the river and showed her how the old miners panned for gold. They tried for two hours without finding a single flake.

All the ranchers went to the Galaxy Cafe for

lunch one day, and Mr. Coker served them himself. Ice cream sundaes for everyone—on the house!

The plan for the Gold Moon shop took shape. The schoolroom would be stocked with all the goods the ranchers planned to sell, and the public would be invited to come on weekends. Julie helped paint signs to advertise the new shop, then went with Allen to hang them on the gate at the end of the drive.

At the end of the second week, Mrs. Albright said it was time she and Julie returned home. Julie felt a stab of loss. She'd miss waking up to the peaceful hush that blanketed the mountain. She'd miss working hard in the cool end-of-summer air and singing songs under the starry night sky. And she was sorry that the ranchers had not solved all their problems. Even Julie's mother was doubtful that the shop would bring in enough money to pay all the taxes the ranchers owed.

"We'll have to think of something else," Uncle

David admitted. "But it's a start."

On the morning they were to leave, Julie and her mother stowed their suitcases in the car, and all the ranchers came outside to see them off. Julie looked around at the ranchers who only two weeks ago were strangers but now felt like family. She wished she could bring her friends CJ and Ivy—and all her friends and their families!—to visit them here at the ranch. They would all love it here! It would be like a fabulous summer camp. A summer camp for families . . .

With that thought, the bud of an idea unfurled. Julie sucked in her breath, her mind racing.

"Time to say good-bye," Mrs. Albright said.

But Julie grabbed her around the waist and spun her around. "Mom!" she exclaimed. "Wait! I know how to save the ranch!"

"Go on then, Viking Julie," Raymond teased, leaning on his crutches. "Tell us!"

Julie tried to speak slowly as all the wonderful

possibilities flashed through her mind. "If you want exciting rides and attractions, you can always go to a theme park, right? But the great thing about Gold Moon Ranch is how peaceful and quiet and beautiful it is. People would pay for that."

She took a deep breath and grinned at them. "So what about turning Gold Moon Ranch into a summer camp for city families? People would come for a taste of your back-to-nature life in the summer. Uncle David could be the camp director—that's a desk job, mostly, right? Jet can teach them about the history of gold mining; Bonnie can show them how to make soap and do laundry the old-fashioned way, and Rose and Aunt Nadine and everybody else will show them how to spin wool and pick vegetables and gather eggs and milk cows and play music under the stars! You can finish shoring up the mine, and you can offer tours! The money you'd earn from the camp—and the new shop—could keep Gold Moon Ranch going."

The ranchers started talking excitedly. Aunt Nadine threw an arm around Julie's shoulders. "What a businesswoman you are," she said. "Just like your mother. It's a fab idea."

"I could be a camp counselor!" said Dolores.

Julie hugged her. "I'll be your first camper."

As Julie and her mom climbed into their car, Aunt Nadine handed Julie a small pouch of felted wool. "Finders keepers," she said. "A souvenir of your first visit to Gold Moon Ranch."

Julie didn't even need to open the pouch. She could feel the weight of the little bottle inside it, heavy in her palm. She thanked Aunt Nadine with a hug, and as their car started down the steep driveway, Julie turned in her seat to wave.

"See you later, City Mouse!" shouted Raymond.

"After a while, Country Mouse," Julie called. "I'll be back for camp next summer!"

INSIDE Julie's World

When Julie was growing up in the 1970s, many young people were frustrated by the problems they saw in the world around them—the war in Vietnam and, closer to home, pollution, greed, poverty, and lifestyles that seemed unhealthy and lacking in meaning and purpose. Some people reacted to these problems by dropping out of mainstream society and forming new communities with other like-minded people. They hoped that these intentional communities, or *communes,* would provide better lives for themselves and their children.

The fictional Gold Moon Ranch is similar to a real commune in Tennessee called The Farm. The founders of The Farm wanted to live in harmony with nature. They wanted to grow their own food and make what they needed instead of depending on things provided by big businesses. They also wanted a peaceful environment for their children. In the 1970s, The Farm had more than a thousand members, making it larger than many small towns. But even idealistic communities like The Farm couldn't provide solutions for some of the bigger problems America was facing.

One of these problems was the plight of soldiers who returned from fighting in Vietnam only to face new kinds of battles at home. Like Raymond's father, many soldiers came back with serious injuries that required long rehabilitation. Some came home to families that had suffered or broken apart during their absence. And instead of being welcomed as heroes, the soldiers were often criticized for having fought in a war that many Americans believed was wrong.

Today, servicemen and -women returning from wars still face difficulties returning to regular life. Countless Americans today still suffer the effects of pollution, poverty, and unhealthy lives. And many Americans still seek a better way of life in intentional communities.

Although few communes like The Farm remain in the United States today, the ideas behind the communes of the 1960s and '70s haven't disappeared. In today's co-housing communities, families live in separate homes but share common areas for meals, work, and get-togethers. In artist communities, artists share land, tools, and work space, and even trade their skills so they can live inexpensively and focus on making art. Senior citizens also join co-housing communities to support one another and share resources as they grow old. All of these communities echo the key idea behind the communes of Julie's time: that people have better lives when they come together and support each other.

Read more of JULIE'S stories,

available from booksellers and at *americangirl.com*

❁ *Classics* ❁

Julie's classic series, now in two volumes:

Volume 1:
The Big Break
Julie's parents' divorce means a new home, a new school, and new friends. Will Julie ever feel at home in her new life?

Volume 2:
Soaring High
As Julie begins to see that change can bring new possibilities, she sets out to make some big changes of her own!

❁ *Journey in Time* ❁

Travel back in time—and spend a day with Julie.

A Brighter Tomorrow
Step back into the 1970s and help Julie win her basketball game, save a stranded sea otter, and clean up the beach! Choose your own path through this multiple-ending story.

❁ *Mysteries* ❁

Suspense and sleuthing with Julie.

The Puzzle of the Paper Daughter: A Julie Mystery
A note written in Chinese leads Julie and Ivy on a search for a long-lost doll.

The Tangled Web: A Julie Mystery
Julie's new friend Carla seems to have the perfect life—but is it *too* good to be true? Worried for Carla, Julie looks for the real story.

A Sneak Peek at

The Tangled Web

A Julie Mystery

Step into another suspenseful adventure
with Julie!

THAT DAY, JULIE invited Carla home with her after school. Julie pushed open the door to Gladrags, her mother's little shop on the ground floor beneath their apartment, and the bell above the door jangled. Carla stepped through the curtain of beads at the shop door, her eyes sparkling. "What a cute place!"

"Gladrags is my mom's baby," Julie said, feeling proud of her mom. Running the shop was a lot of work, but a lot of fun, too. It was a treasure trove of trendy miscellany: There were racks of Indian print dresses, knitted ponchos, colorful silk scarves, and hand-tooled leather belts. There were glass cases displaying earrings, necklaces, and bracelets, and baskets of charms and beads for making your own. Shelves around the room held pottery and candles, incense, kites, lamps, and wooden toys. A table in the window was full of hand-painted flowerpots, and macramé plant holders hung from the ceiling.

But today there was no sign of Mrs. Albright. Instead, Hank was working behind the counter. He waved to Julie and Carla. "Hello, lovely ladies. The boss has gone off with Tracy at the wheel and left me in charge. They shouldn't be gone too long—just went to the market to buy provisions for our Thanksgiving feast." He smiled at them. "The fellows I'm bringing with me to the party will just be so glad of a home-cooked meal, I doubt they'll notice whether we're eating roast turkey or plain old hot dogs."

"I think it'll be fun to have the soldiers with us on Thanksgiving," Julie said. Then she introduced Carla. "This is Carla—she's new at school. Carla, this is our friend Hank. He works at the rehab center for injured soldiers."

Carla winced. "That must be so hard," she murmured, and then quickly turned away to look at some silver bangles displayed on top of the counter. She tried one on her wrist.

"Two for a buck," Hank said. "Pretty, aren't they?"

"Yes!" Carla hesitated, then put the bracelet back. "I'll come back when I've got my money with me."

Julie led the way up the stairs at the back of the shop. "I'll be down here till your mom gets back," Hank called after them. "She said she left you a snack on the table."

Julie and Carla hurried up to the kitchen, where a plate of Oreos waited. They each took three cookies and headed for Julie's room.

Carla was good company. She roamed around, inspecting the bead curtain around Julie's bed, her bulletin board, her posters, her bookshelf, and the framed photo of Julie and her sister sitting on the buckboard of an old-fashioned covered wagon.

"That picture was taken last summer," Julie told Carla, "on the last leg of a cross-country trip to celebrate the Bicentennial. We had loads of fun living like pioneers!"

"Sounds cool," said Carla. She plopped herself

cross-legged in the center of Julie's bed, as if she'd been Julie's friend forever, and Julie smiled. "My family has had some great trips together, too," Carla said. She described the amazing vacations she'd taken with her large family: They'd gone to Hawaii, Canada, Mexico, and Italy. Julie couldn't help feeling a twinge of envy; the Bicentennial trip had been wonderful, but her family rarely went traveling, and never all together since the divorce. Her mom had to work so hard running Gladrags, and her dad's busy flight schedule kept him away often.

A little later, Julie and Carla made popcorn, shaking the foil-covered Jiffy-Pop pan over the stove and watching as the foil puffed up like a balloon. They talked about what they liked to read and discovered they both loved mysteries.

"I named my spider Harriet, in honor of Harriet the Spy," said Julie. "She's Harriet the Spy-der!"

"*Ew*—you have a pet spider?"

"Only because I really want a dog, but I can't

have one," Julie explained.

"Well . . . my sister is named for Nancy Drew!" Carla told her, giggling. "No, really she was named for our Aunt Nancy. Nancy is my kindergarten sister. She can be a pest sometimes. At least my dog doesn't sneak into my room and play with my stuff."

"What kind of dog do you have?" Julie asked eagerly.

"A border collie," said Carla. "And he's *super* smart." She told Julie about all the tricks her dog could do. He could shake paws and jump over hurdles, roll over and play dead, and even search for hidden objects.

"You have to invite me over to meet him!" cried Julie. "We could hide things for him to find."

"Or I could bring him by when I'm taking him on a walk," offered Carla. "You could walk with us."

"I'd love to!"

The girls took their popcorn back to Julie's room. Julie got out her tape recorder. "Okay," she said into the microphone, "this is KJC radio. Today we present an interview with—*ta-dah!*—Carla Warner, New Girl in Town."

Carla laughed. "What's KJC stand for?"

"Well, West Coast radio stations always start with K. And the J is for Julie, of course, and the C—"

"—is for Carla!" finished Carla. "That's good. Or we could call it KSPY. Because we both like spies."

"That's even better," said Julie, rewinding the cassette tape. "I'll start over." She spoke dramatically into the microphone. "This is KSPY, best station in the West. And today's interview features the famous Carla Warner, New Spy in Town!"

About the Author

As a girl, KATHRYN REISS always enjoyed reading stories about the California Gold Rush. She loved reading mysteries, too, and started writing them because nothing very exciting or sinister ever happened in her own neighborhood. Now she lives with her family in a big old house in a small town near San Francisco, and likes to escape to the mountains whenever she can. Her novels of suspense for children and teens have won many awards. She is a professor of English at Mills College and is always hard at work on a new story.